PROJECT APEX II: ERADICATION

Michael Bray

"We are a plague on the Earth."

- David Attenborough

"Hence the end of the world should be awaited with all longing by all believers."

- William Ames

"Life could do nothing for her, beyond giving time for a better preparation for death."

— Jane Austen

CHAPTER ONE

AIR FORCE ONE CRASH SITE

WEST VIRGINIA

WASHINGTON DC, USA

It was Armageddon. At no point in the history of mankind had simultaneous coordinated attacks caused such destruction. The death of the President was incidental to the devastating news of the nuclear strikes. As word of the unthinkable events filtered through to news agencies and media outlets, there was doubt about their validity. Many of the reports were too awful to comprehend, let alone believe possible. Soon enough, the truth filtered through and induced a global sense of fear. Tokyo had been reduced to dust along with many of its near thirteen million residents, the sun blocked out by thick black clouds of ash and pulverised concrete, which hung in the air and reduced visibility to nothing. In Paris, the devastation was just as effective. Fires devoured the city as those outside the blast radius descended into a confused panic, unable to comprehend that their city had been attacked or what they should do to stay safe. Many hunkered down and waited for the government to intervene and tell them what to do, unaware that there was no government, the nation left in tatters, its leadership wiped out in one blow. The final bomb landed in Berlin where more than half a million people had their existence ended in the centre of the near half mile blast zone, a flash of white light followed by the searing heat the only awareness they had before their lives were extinguished. It was the single most devastating coordinated attack on humanity in history, a cataclysmic event which would never be forgotten. All over the world, people huddled around television screens, frightened and wondering if they were next. Others tried to hide. Vacating to basements with their families and waiting for that flash of light which would signal their deaths.

The fear became desperation, and society imploded with little resistance. Citizens of major cities the world over fell into panic and asked questions of their governments and world leaders, people who they believed were in control and had the answers. This situation, however, was much bigger than elections or war and it soon became apparent that no answers were coming, for the leaders of the world themselves were in disarray, each country a melting pot of chaos as old tensions were forgotten for the greater good of trying to find and share information about what was happening in the world. The countries bordering those hit by the nuclear bombs were put on high alert to receive those who were evacuating the affected cities in their thousands as medical care and temporary accommodation was requested. Despite drills and scenarios practised in the event of such a disaster the world was unprepared for what was happening. Even those living outside the disaster zones were affected. Ruptured gas lines caused thousands of individual fires across hundreds of miles, burning through homes and offices, stores and warehouses. Power grids were destroyed and left hundreds of thousands without precious electricity, dealing another hammer blow to the civilised world. In Washington, the wreckage of Air Force One burned, sending thick, black smoke rolling into the air from its scattered remains. Four buildings around the impact site were in flames, the streets littered with debris. Seats had been thrown through shop windows and still contained the blackened remains of passengers. An enormous engine had embedded itself into the side of a glass-fronted office building, the shattered lobby now a billion tiny mirrors reflecting the flames. A section of undercarriage had obliterated a red pickup truck which was side on in the middle of the street, its suspension broken, its driver crushed inside the cab, his face mangled against the steering wheel. Worse still were the bodies.

Charred husks of meat were strewn over the debris field, the force of the crash tearing them to pieces. Even that paled in comparison to the pieces which had been thrown far enough from the heat of the flames to still be recognisable. A chewed up hand still wearing a wedding ring. A foot, the shoe still tied, the brown leather still polished. Police and fire crews arrived on the scene, trying to quell the flames with arcing jets of water. There was no search for survivors. It was clear they had attended a mission of recovery rather than rescue. As the fire crews attempted to control the blaze and keep the watching crowds back, men clad in expensive suits and dark sunglasses arrived in SUV's with opaque windows. Flashing their government identification, they pushed to the front of the crowd and right into the inner circle where the firefighters battled to control the blaze.

"You need to get out of here," The fire chief said, shouting above the roar of fire and symphony of sirens. He was a thin man with a salty moustache and regarded the new arrivals with barely hidden contempt.

"Special Agent Jones," the man barked back, snapping open his identification. "We're here to contain the scene and recover the president's body."

"There's nothing to recover," The fire chief shot back, locking eyes with the agent. "So far all we found are pieces of people."

Jones shifted, digesting the information. "But you don’t know for sure, Air Force One wasn’t just a regular aircraft, it had an armoured fuselage and-"

"Pal, just take a look for yourself," the chief said, flicking an exasperated arm towards the burning, twisted wreckage. "We're not looking for survivors. I've been in this game a long time. As much as I hate to say it, if the president was on board, then he's gone."

Jones didn't react, at first, he stared at the fire chief and then looked at the wreckage. People behind the taped-off area heard this exchange and reported back to friends. Posts were made on social media, news outlets were alerted. Like a wave, word spread, and the public perception of events took a very noticeable shift. People were no longer viewing things as something going on elsewhere in the world. Like a slow growing cancer, the fear spread. The people understood that the streets were no longer a safe place. As the crowds disbursed, Jones turned to his men, who waited at his back.

"Someone get me the Vice President on the line. I need to speak with him."

Jones strode back towards the crowd, which was thinning as people made their way to what they hoped was safety. The fire chief watched Jones go, then with a shake of the head, went back to his job. Like the rest of his men, he was afraid and wasn't sure what was going to happen next.

CHAPTER TWO

Draven, Kate & Herman

McNair Road, Virginia,

USA

They had seen the plane go down from Kate's car, which was stuck in the endless snake of unmoving traffic which glittered and shimmered under the gaze of the early afternoon sun. They were too far away to identify the markings of the presidential jet and assumed it was a commercial plane. As he watched the smoke roll into the sky in the distance, Draven realised he was holding his breath and let it out in a long, slow exhalation.

"That was done on purpose," he said, glancing at Kate.

"Hijack?"

"Maybe," Draven said. "People are going crazy enough as is without terrorists to contend with. They're scared."

"I'm scared."

Draven looked at Kate and wondered why he couldn't see it before. Behind the determination, he could see the disbelief.

"The sooner we get to the Pentagon, the better," he said, finding it was the best he could do under the circumstances. He glanced at Herman in the back seat, who was frowning, white earphones plugged in, phone clutched in his hand. Herman caught Draven watching, and blinked as if waking from a particularly vivid dream.

"You okay?" Draven said.

Herman pulled out one of his earpieces and looked at both Kate and Draven. "Turn on the radio," he said.

"What station?"

"Any," Herman replied.

Kate flicked on the radio and turned up the volume. They sat in silence, listening to the news coming in from all over the world about the nuclear attacks. It was then, as the three of them sat in the sun-baked car that something changed. A shift in the atmosphere. Draven tried to think of a word to describe it and found his vocabulary didn't contain one. Fear was too weak, as were horror, terror, and disbelief. For the first time since he had been picked up in Mexico, Draven questioned how safe his family was. He took his phone out of his pocket, went to the phone book and dialled the number for Leanne. The number didn't connect. He tried again with the same result.

Kate looked at him across the seat. "Everything alright?"

"I can't reach my family. I want to tell them to get somewhere safe."

"Your family? I thought you didn't have any. You said you were unmarried"

"I'm divorced. I thought this thing was isolated here, but it seems like I was wrong. Now I want to get in touch and tell her to get somewhere safe."

Kate handed him her phone. "Here, try mine."

Draven held one phone in each hand, transferring the number from his handset to Kate's then alternatively trying to dial through on each. "No answer. I can't even get a connection."

"Networks are probably down. Try not to panic." Kate said.

"I should have contacted them before. Why the hell didn't I tell them to get to safety sooner?"

"You can't beat yourself up over this. Things have

been crazy."

"That's not the point. I still should have made contact. My kids....." he trailed off, his brain throwing up every awful scenario imaginable.

"How many children do you have?" Kate asked.

"Two. Here, let me show you." He took his wallet out of his jeans and opened it. Inside the plastic window in the front was a photograph of two children, both smiling and bearing an eerie resemblance to Draven. He turned it towards Kate so she could see. "The boy there, he's Ethan. He just turned seven a couple of months ago."

"Cute kid," Kate said.

Draven nodded. "And that's my daughter, Imogen. She's eleven now. Damn, they grow up so fast." He frowned and snapped the wallet closed, then tried the phones again.

"What happened, if you don't mind me asking?" Kate said.

"Well, Leanne and I were young when we met. A little too young to marry and start a family, both of which we did against the advice of our families. We were young and impulsive. We didn't know what love was, never mind if we were in it. For a while things were great. When Imogen came along she was a distraction away from our own problems that had started to take over our lives. See my job meant I had to be away travelling. The hours were long and because I wanted a future for the family, I didn't turn down any overtime. I guess she got lonely and started to resent me. I don't blame her now, I can see why she would do that. At the time, though, my reaction was to hate her back. We were close to getting divorced when we found out she was pregnant with Ethan. We hoped it would be enough to fix things, but if anything it made it worse. With one child and another on the way, I had to work even harder and she felt more alone and isolated. We split when Ethan was three. The divorce was finalised a few months later."

"Do you still speak?"

Draven shook his head. "The divorce was hard on all of us. She moved away to a little town on the English coast. I came over here, hoping the distance would help."

"So when do you see your children?"

Draven couldn't look at her when he replied. He was too embarrassed. "I don't. I speak to them on the phone when I can and send them presents for Christmas and their birthday, but I don't physically see much of them. I'm not proud of it, but its easier this way."

"I'm sorry."

"Me too. Now all I care about is getting in contact with them and making sure they get somewhere safe."

"When we get to the Pentagon, I'll get someone to make contact. Don't worry, we'll make sure they are safe."

"Thank you, I appreciate it."

"We need to be getting a move on, though. We don't seem to be making any progress."

"No, I noticed that. Hang on." He wound down the window and stuck his head out, enabling him to see further down the long snake of cars. He could see the reason for their lack of progress. Many of the vehicles had been abandoned, doors left ajar, belongings forgotten. People walked alone or stood and talked in groups by the side of the road, faces pale, eyes wide, mouths open as they wandered in a daze and discussed the unbelievable news. Draven wondered how many would survive, how many of these strangers who walked past the car like ghoulish spectres thrust into the harsh light of day would get to see their families again in a world which was rapidly unravelling around them.

It was a sobering thought and one which made him aware that they needed to take action.

"We can't stay here," Draven heard himself say from some distant place as he pulled his head back into the car. "This line of traffic is going nowhere."

"Then we go on foot. It's only a couple of miles and we can cut through Arlington cemetery and go cross country."

"Alright, let's get moving. The sooner we get there, the sooner we can get in touch with my family."

Kate grabbed his arm, and this time, there was no mistake. She was afraid. "Do you think any more nukes will be launched?" He wished he could have told her a lie if only to put her mind at ease, but the truth was he didn't have it in him. "I don't know. This is a game changer."

"You're telling me. I never expected it would get this bad."

"None of us did. This is a bold move." Draven said, watching as a mother and young child walked past the car towards a future that was uncertain.

"Alright then, let's get to it," Kate replied, climbing out of the car. Draven and Herman joined her, leaving the car behind with the others as they set out on foot.

Draven realised he hadn't appreciated how gridlocked the traffic was. It stretched in both directions as far as he could see. They veered off McNair Road and walked towards the tree line of the woodland which bordered Arlington Cemetery. "Do you think that's the end of it?" Kate asked.

Draven looked at her as they walked, unsure if she was aware she had just asked an almost identical question. He suspected she was in shock and couldn't blame her. He was struggling too. He took a second glance, taking the time to take in the details. Her profile was cast in gold by the sun. He ticked off the plus points in his mind. Strong jaw, good cheekbones. Wonderful deep eyes which he was sure would look spectacular if not for the fear inside them. It occurred to him that under less horrific circumstances, he could be attracted to her. "The end of what?" he asked, deciding not to remind her that they had already had this conversation.

"The nukes."

"Best if we don't think too much about that. We need to deal with the here and now. If it helps, I think we at least should be safe here. In fact, I think we're in the safest place to be right now. It stands to reason that

Joshua wouldn't want to launch anything so devastating quite so close to home. Try to relax a little"

"It's not him I'm worried about, it's the retaliation that might come from other countries in the confusion," she muttered.

Draven hadn't even considered a retaliatory attack, and a chill brushed down his spine despite the warmth of the day as he saw snapshots of in his mind of awful scenarios involving his children. "Do you think that's a possibility? Especially with everything that's happened?"

"I'd like to think not," Kate replied. "I just worry that some of the other countries who have been looking for a reason to go to war with us might see this as a valid reason to attack."

"Oh, man," Herman muttered, one earphone still wedged in place. "It's just been on the radio. The President's dead."

"What?" Kate and Draven said in unison.

"It's just been confirmed. That plane we saw go down was Air Force One. No survivors. This is fucked up, man." He was agitated and scratched his cheek.

“One of them was on the plane,” Draven said.

“One of who?”

“Joshua’s men. You saw how it crashed. Nose down. Aimed deliberately. It has to be related.”

“I’m not disagreeing with you. I just don’t understand.” None of them did, and so they walked without speaking for a while, finally getting some relief from the heat of the day by passing into the shadow of the trees and the woods beyond. Like a wall, a dense silence fell around them as the sounds of the city were muted.

"I don’t understand," Kate said as they made their way through the trees. "Why would they do this? Why go so far to cause so much destruction?"

"Fear," Herman said as he bobbed along behind them, hands thrust in pockets. "It's an age old tactic used by dictators all over the world. Keep the people frightened, make them believe they can’t think for themselves and most of the time they will follow like well-behaved sheep."

"Enough with the conspiracy crap," Kate sighed, unable to even muster any anger.

"No, he's right," Draven said. "I think that's exactly what's happening. Rule by fear. It’s a classic dictator tactic, and now he’s done this, Joshua is in a hell of a position to have the majority of people do what he says."

"Why, though? What is he trying to prove?"

"That I don’t know. Whatever it is, it seems he's planned for it and is executing it perfectly. I think whatever happens from here on, things will never be the same again."

They moved on, each happy with their own thoughts for a while. Sometimes, it was just better that way.

CHAPTER THREE

Presidential office

The Pentagon,

USA

Paul Carter paced, hands clasped behind his back after just being sworn in as President. He had waited for such a moment for as long as he could remember and yet felt somehow cheated. He didn't want to take over the country in the middle of a global crisis. He had always hoped for a quiet, trouble free presidency much like that of his predecessor, however, it seemed he was going to get nothing even remotely like it. The devastation of the nuclear attacks was still sinking in, as were the repercussions which would be felt for years to come. Worse, and more disturbing than the lootings, the fires, the riots, the destruction and the overall crumbling of society were the reports coming in of the dead coming back to life. When he had first been told, he had actually laughed, remembering back to when he was a young boy watching George Romero's Dawn of the Dead. The genre of movies spawned a cult following, one which had seen a resurgence of late. Books, television programmes and movies covered the possibility of the dead coming back to life, and yet it was never something anyone believed possible.

Zombie.

He hated the word. It was one that every report he had received about them, both written and oral, had failed to use. He supposed it was for the same reason he had trouble with it. Zombie implied something born from fiction, something made up by fiction writers which couldn't exist in the real world.

"Zombie."

He whispered it to himself in his office, the word sounding flat and lifeless as it left his lips.

No.

He couldn't use that word. He couldn't imagine the reaction from the public if people started to scream it on his say so, not that it mattered. He knew he was in an impossible situation. No matter what name the government gave to the phenomenon, people would still call them zombies. It was the go-to word, and to be fair, it was the best description for what they were, even if it wasn’t one the government was prepared to use. Fortunately, the public wasn't aware of the problem yet. The nuclear bombs and the death of the president had caused enough confusion and distraction to keep people’s focus away from it, which, however awful, was a small mercy. It was only a matter of time until somebody realised what was happening, and so he would approach it head on and let the public know what they were facing rather than waiting until people started to die.

A knock on the door broke his train of thought, as his assistant, a jittery barrel of a man called Bill Watson, strode into the room.

"What is it, Bill?"

"Mr. President, we just received word that both the Russian president and Italian prime minister have been assassinated. Attempts were made on the British and Dutch leaders but they survived."

"Our friends in the White House?" Carter said as he perched on the edge of his desk and rubbed his temples.

"Yes, Sir.”

“Is someone out looking for them?”

“No, sir. We don’t have the resources right now.”

“Jesus Christ this is a nightmare. What else?”

Watson cleared this throat and wrung his hands. “Sir, we have widespread reports of civilians becoming infected and changing in major cities across the country. This is getting out of control."

"Jesus Christ. This is Fitzgerald’s fault. He should have acted when this first became a problem. Now he's left me to clean up his damn mess."

Watson said nothing, knowing it wasn’t his place to remind the new president that his former namesake had paid for his error with his life. Carter stood and walked to the painting on the wall of a Spanish vineyard, wishing he was there soaking up the expertly painted sun without a care in the world. "Do we have the death toll from the nuclear attacks yet?" he asked without turning away from the painting

"Estimates only, sir. It's chaos out there."

"So give me the numbers."

"Well, conservative estimates at the blast zones are anything around-"

"No, I don’t want conservative. Worst case scenario." He snapped, turning to face his Chief of Staff.

Watson cleared his throat. "Well, sir, taking into account fallout and density of population in the impact zones, we could be looking at up to twenty million dead."

"Twenty million? Jesus, this is worse than I thought. Twenty million…."

"That's not all, sir."

"Go on."

"The situation with the, uh, dead sir. It's getting out of control. We have reports of this happening all over the country. We don't have the resources to contain it."

"Reports are no good for me Watson, I need confirmation. Get a team out there and bring one of these... reanimates in. Test it. Find out what the hell makes it tick so we can stop it."

"Is that the term we're using sir, uh...Reanimates?" Watson asked.

"It's better than damn zombie. I need CDC in on this too, give them everything they need to figure this out. I want to know how infectious they are, how they work, how we can kill them. I also want the army mobilised and out on the streets. They're authorised to use lethal force if necessary to keep the peace. That goes for hostiles and civilians. People are rioting and looting out there and we need to keep control. This country will not fall apart on my watch."

"Yes, Sir."

Carter was shaking, partly from rage, a little through fear. "Get me a video conference with the world leaders. Make sure it's a secure line. I think it's clear that borders and politics don't mean anything now. This is a fight we're in together. I hope they see it the same way"

"I'll see who we can get, sir. As you can imagine, the rest of the world is as bogged down in this as we are."

"I understand that. Just do your best,"

"What about the White House sir? Are there plans to recapture it?" Watson asked.

"Have we made any headway on recapturing control of our nuclear weapons?" Carter asked.

"No, sir. Whoever they used to hack into our systems have locked us out. The physical launch sites have also been compromised as have the destroyers in the Gulf of Mexico. We've lost control of our arsenal."

"Then the White House isn't a priority. The last thing I want is to give these pricks an excuse to drop more nukes. Just please tell me we have something in the works that might give us a chance against these bastards."

"Actually, we do, or at least, we might. We have an

agent inbound with a civilian who is supposed to be the next best expert on this after Genaro. He was the one who first discovered the species of monkey which were the basis of the Apex project research."

"Alright, I want to see him when he gets here. We need to get a grip on this, Bill. I refuse to go down in history as the president who oversaw the end of the world. Get the army down there doing their job. If people get out of line, they are authorised to use force to maintain order."

“Sir, President Fitzgerald thought-"

"President Fitzgerald is dead," Carter spat. "I'm in charge now and I’m not about to make the same mistake as he did by sitting on my hands and watching the world burn around me. Now call it a zombie, the undead, a reanimate or whatever you want. Just get one of them off the streets, cut it up and find a way to stop it."

"Yes sir," Watson said, making his leave.

Carter sat at his desk, inhaling as the soft leather took him into its embrace. His hands were shaking. He was clinging on to control by his fingertips and knew if he was to keep the faith of the people and his staff, he would need to make a series of tough decisions which might well prove unpopular, but necessary all the same. It was no longer a game of political posturing and gaining public popularity to ensure another term in office. He was up to his neck in a battle for the survival of the human race, and it was one he had no intention of losing.

II

As President Carter paced his office and the world fell into chaos, the next phase of Joshua's plan was put into action.

In the Atlantic Ocean, the U.S.S Bombardier was already under the control of the small team of Joshua's men who had stowed away on board. Systematically, the ten-strong team had worked through the boat, maiming all within its network of narrow corridors bow to stern, top to bottom. With smoke lingering thick and heavy in its corridors and the bodies of its dead crew lying where they fell, the new team in charge of the vessel fired a missile into the air. On deck, the crew watched as the trail of smoke grew less and less visible as the projectile climbed ever higher.

Just outside the atmosphere of the earth, a vast

floating junkyard orbited the planet, a sad and disturbing testament to mankind's lack of care for their environment. Space shuttle debris from various missions floated in perpetual orbits, destined to live as evidence of the uncaring legacy of man long after the species had become extinct. Amid this floating mass of debris, were the various satellites required for the world to communicate. Everything from governments to telecommunications companies had launched them into space, where they sent and relayed information to their respective countries the world over. The first of the missiles struck home on one of the many American governed satellites, obliterating it and severing the communication abilities of the Americans. For the next five hours, the battleship fired missile after missile, bringing down satellites owned by the Chinese, Russians and British. Even the telecommunication satellites weren't spared, their destruction blacking out mobile phone coverage followed by television satellites responsible for broadcasting television pictures to homes all over the world.

In one act, Joshua sent a world which was reliant on technology back to the Stone Age.

CHAPTER FOUR

The Apex virus had a different effect on women. Whereas the virus increased the testosterone levels of men, in women it increased their fertility. As part of his plan to repopulate the earth with his own superior species, Joshua had given orders for camps to be set up within hours of their assault on the White House, places where human prisoners could be placed to work for their superior evolutionary masters. Much like the Nazi concentration camps of the Second World War, people were captured on the streets by Joshua's men and herded in like sheep, forced to work in barely humane conditions until they were physically and mentally broken as they sourced materials to construct the camps in the locations chosen prior to Joshua's assault on humanity. The brief for Joshua's men was simple. Destroy the sick, disabled and old, capture the young and strong. Some camps would be built from scratch using new materials, others would be set up in existing facilities, repurposed for the grand scheme Joshua had set into play. Joshua's men had been efficient in their orders, killing without mercy and rounding up terrified citizens as the authorities fought in vain to stop them. Smouldering piles of bodies littered the streets as Joshua's men rampaged murdered and raped with abandon, easily pushing back police and army resistance, each victory resulting in them changing more to their own kind, and commandeering weaponry and vehicles with which to continue spreading their plague. Local authorities, unable to communicate on anything but short wave radio, were thrown into disarray. Many had lost the will to fight, returning to families in the hope of ensuring their own safety. The ones who remained were outnumbered and outgunned.

The first camp went up in northern Canada against the bitter cold backdrop of barren snow-covered wastelands. Unlike their genetically enhanced captors who didn't feel the cold, for those who were transported to the bleak open plains, the chill bit hard enough to almost make them forget how afraid they were. Adults and children alike huddled together in fear of what was to come. Lumber was transported in flatbed trucks to the camp locations, which were, in turn, circled by the infected, who had commandeered weapons and vehicles to oversee construction and ensure nobody could escape. Men and children were put to work on constructing cabins in which to sleep when the day's backbreaking work was done. Others set to digging great pits into the earth, deep holes where unbeknownst to them, the dead and those deemed useless would be tossed in their hundreds of thousands in the coming days before they could come back. Although Dr. Genaro knew how they returned to life, they were uncontrollable, mindless beasts driven on by its parasite to bite the nearest living thing it could in order to pass its seed onto a new host. The ones which didn't manage to find a host wandered perpetually, the virus keeping the vital functions of the brain alive just enough to operate the extremities and allow the host to shamble in search of a victim. Even though the virus could keep the body alive, it could not stop the process of decay. Some of the dead had already started to putrefy as organs settled, the gasses causing the stomach to bloat. Skin started to discolour and crack at the joints. Eyes became milky, unsighted globes staring ahead as the virus drove its decomposing vessel in search of a new host.

Other camps were set up around factories and steel

mills which were heavily fortified by the ever growing armies and filled with terrified prisoners who had been snatched from the streets. Under Joshua's orders, the women were separated from the men and placed into bespoke facilities for the sole purpose of breeding. All captured women of birthing age were to be infected with the virus, then have their heads shaved and placed into shackles. Under Joshua's orders, their old identities were to be forgotten. All of them from the day they were taken would be named simply as Eve, and would have to endure the horror of repeated and violent rape by Joshua's men until pregnancy occurred. This horrific practice was Joshua's plan to introduce the first natural births of their new race. Within the first days, thousands of women scattered across the globe would endure such violent and degrading brutality as Joshua enforced his plan with the ruthless determination he was becoming notorious for. Those who had been captured prayed for help, for someone to come and save them from the nightmare they were being forced to live.

In the wider world, however, the assembly of the camps went unnoticed amid the chaos of the nuclear explosions and the crumbling of society as Joshua's men rampaged and bit and changed those they deemed worthy, and savaged and murdered those they did not. In their desperation, people turned on each other, reverting to the primal savagery which humanity had learned to forget since they became a civilised species. Smoke hung heavy in the air, a blanket of haze which smelled of burning flesh.

In the bullet-ridden shell of the White House, Joshua looked out over his domain.

CHAPTER FIVE

Draven, Kate & Herman

Arlington, Virginia

USA

Kate led them through the woods towards the Pentagon, which was just at the opposite end of the cemetery.

"Internet's down," Herman grunted as he shoved his phone in his jacket pocket and moved alongside Draven, matching his pace.

"Could be the reception under the tree cover," Draven replied. He had long since given up on trying to get through to his family by phone and was relying on Kate getting him some help at the Pentagon.

"Probably been shut down," Herman grunted. "Did you know you shouldn't access the internet by phone? The governments monitor it. They activate the handset speaker remotely and listen in to everything you say. They can even use the camera to take pictures. Big

Brother is always watching, man. A buddy of mine told me."

Kate glared at Herman but said nothing. Draven couldn't help but smile. "Well, maybe you can ask them about it yourself when we reach the Pentagon. Just be careful they don't lock you up for spreading government secrets."

"Hey that's not funny, man, that's not funny at all."

"Sorry, I was just messing with you."

"I thought you believed in this stuff I-"

"Shh."

Draven and Herman both stopped speaking and looked ahead. Beyond Kate was a blue domed tent. Outside were boxes and supplies and a portable camping stove. Beside the tent stood a brute of a man, all shoulders and beard. He was dressed in a khaki jacket and had a black beanie hat pulled down to the top of his eyebrows. Behind him, peering out from behind his legs like frightened deer, were a small boy and a girl, and beyond them, half in and half out of the tent was a woman who Draven presumed was the man's wife. The man was pointing a hunting rifle at them.

"I don't want no trouble," he said as his wife climbed out of the tent and threw a protective arm around her children.

"Hey, take it easy, we don't either," Draven said, noticing the man's jacket and face was splattered with blood.

"This is our spot. You can't be here." He grunted, adjusting his grip on the gun.

"Sir, I work for the United States government. You are impeding us. Lower your weapon and step aside." Kate cut in.

"You back off!" he shrieked.

"Kate, take it easy," Draven said, keeping a close eye on the rifle, then looking the man in the eye. "Hey, what's your name?"

"None of your fuckin' business," The man snapped. Draven could see he was frightened, which meant he was only a scare away from pulling the trigger.

"Please, I'm just trying to show you we're good people. My name's Richard. This is Kate and our friend Herman. As we said, we're just passing through."

"That's what the guy on the road said."

"What guy?" Draven said, keeping his tone neutral.

"The guy who took our car. He looked like a nice guy, like you, but he put a gun in my wife's face and stole our van. Now we're stuck here."

"Alan please, maybe we should listen to them," the man's wife said from his shoulder.

"Alan? Is that your name?" Draven asked.

The man nodded.

"Okay. Look, I understand what you're going through, I do. Whatever that other person did, I promise you, we won't do that."

"I shot him," Alan blurted, his lip quivering before he took in a great gulp of air and clenched his teeth. "I had no choice. All our stuff was in the back. We would have died. I tried to warn him, I tried to tell him, but I had no choice. I... I killed him."

Draven risked a glance at Kate, but she didn't return it; instead she was tense, watching the man carefully, her eyes sharp and aware.

"Look," Draven said, turning back to the man. "With everything that's happening it's understandable that you're tense and looking out for your family. I understand that. I have a family of my own that I'm trying to make sure are safe. If you'll just lower your weapon, we'll be on our way and nobody has to get hurt, okay?

"Don't patronise me. You think I'm an idiot? That guy thought I was an idiot too until I shot him, and now

I have his damn brains all over me. Worse is that I damaged the car. Maybe a bullet went into the engine or something, I don't know. Either way, we had to come out here on foot. We're not hurting anyone, we just want to wait this thing out."

"I know, I get it."

"All you need to know is I'll do whatever it takes to protect my family. Keep that in mind."

Draven licked his lips, choosing each word with care. "Look, Alan, I understand what you're going through. You're scared, I'm scared too, but you can't stay here. It's not safe."

"Nowhere is," he said, sighing the words. "Have you seen what's happening out there? You can't stay in the cities, people are on the rampage. It doesn't take much for the looters to come out and riots to start. Forget the authorities too. Police are no good, they're overrun trying to keep everyone in order. No, we can't rely on anyone else to help us. We'll be fine here by ourselves."

"I get that, but you haven't thought this through."

"What do you know about it?"

"How will you survive? How will you eat? Please, I know about this stuff, about living off the land. I'm trying to help you." Draven said, taking a cautious step closer.

"Back, get the fuck back or I swear to god I'll put a bullet in you."

The split second of distraction was all Kate needed. She drew her weapon, adjusting her stance and aiming it at Alan's face with the poise and confidence afforded by her training. "Put the gun down now sir," she said, her voice flat and robotic.

"Back off! I warned you!" Alan replied as his family shrank against him.

"Kate, I'm handling this," Draven said through gritted teeth, thinking it would be a miracle if any of them came out of the situation alive.

"We don't have time for this bullshit," she snapped.

"Please, just put the gun down. Let me handle this."

"You better listen to him, listen to what he's sayin'," Alan said, clearly rattled and afraid.

"Sir," Kate said, ignoring both Draven and Alan's pleas. "You are interfering in a government operation which is vital to the security of this country. If you don't lower your weapon, I'll be forced to open fire. I have authority to take your life if you further impede our progress."

"Kate, this is insane!" Draven said, sensing the

standoff was about to get out of control.

"You can shoot me if you have to. I'll do whatever it takes to protect my family." Alan wailed, eyes flicking towards Draven then back to Kate.

"Sir, the best thing you can do for your family is to lower the weapon. I won’t ask you again."

"You're bluffing,"

"I don’t bluff, sir. If you want proof of that, just keep pointing that gun at me."

"Alan, please put the gun down and we can take you with us. We're heading for the Pentagon. They can protect you there, you and your family." Draven said.

"Why should I believe you?" Alan replied, the hesitation in his voice telling Draven he'd struck a chord.

"It's the government. They have a duty to protect its citizens. You'll be safer if you come with us."

“As if we could just walk in there. You think nobody else has thought of going there for help?”

“We have clearance, the highest level. We can get you in.” Draven said, taking a step closer to Alan.

“You better not be lying,” Alan said, lowering the gun. “I’m a good man, this isn’t what I wanted my kids to see.”

“I know, I understand. Just come along with us. You don’t have to be scared anymore.”

"You promise you'll take us?" he said, letting the gun fall to his side.

"Absolutely."

"Alright," he said, letting the gun fall to his side and raising his other arm in surrender.

"Kate?" Draven said quietly. "He's done as you asked. Put the gun away."

"Get the rifle from him. I don’t want him pointing it at us as soon as I put my gun down," she said, still flat, still robotic.

Draven walked towards Alan appreciating how tall he was up close, and how afraid he and his family were. "It's okay," he said as he took the rifle, giving his family a reassuring half-smile. “Just relax.”

He returned to Kate’s side, surprised to see she was still aiming her weapon at the family. "Okay, it's done. Now put the gun away and let's go."

"Wait, we need to pack up our stuff," Alan said.

"No. We can't take you."

All eyes went to Kate, who was staring straight at Alan, a defiance Draven hadn’t noticed before in her eyes.

“You promised you’d help us," Alan said to Draven.

"Why can’t we take them with us? They need our help." Draven said.

"We're on a mission. We don’t have time to babysit civilians."

"You can’t just leave them out here. They're vulnerable," Draven hissed.

"The entire world is vulnerable. Think of the bigger picture here."

"We have a duty to help." Draven snapped.

"No, we have a duty to figure out how to fix this problem," she said, striding forward. "Come on, we don’t have much time."

“I promised them help.”

She looked at him then, eyes intense and full of fire. “It wasn’t up to you to promise anything.”

Draven looked at Alan, the hate and betrayal in the strangers face impossible to ignore. He lowered his head. Kate glanced at Herman, seeing he too was disgusted. He spat in the dirt and watched her turn towards the trees. “Come on, we’re wasting time,” she said as she walked away. With no other option, Herman and Draven followed Kate into the woods. Draven took a last look over his shoulder at them, wishing he could explain or tell them something and seeing only hatred. For the first time, as they walked into the woods and left Alan and his family behind, Draven wondered if Joshua's idea of eradicating the human species might not be such a bad one after all.

CHAPTER SIX

CHURCH OF HOLY RIGHTEOUSNESS

DALLAS, TEXAS

An overcast day greeted Fisher as he stared out over his three-acre farm. He exhaled, and adjusted his tie, reminding himself that the chaos of the world was no reason to have a tardy appearance. He had seen people who had used the apocalypse as an excuse to stop caring about themselves, but not Fisher. Appearance was everything, even more now that people would be looking to him as a leader. He picked up his bible and clutched it to his chest. He believed in the good word of God. Trusted it, just the way his father had.

His father had been a good man, fierce and determined, a real pillar of the community. Miles could remember him well, a big man with a booming voice and thick black beard. He ruled by fear, and although the public image he gave off was one of a gentle, caring man, behind closed doors, he ruled with cast iron discipline, ensuring that both he had Earl learned that to go against his wishes was to mean not being able to sit for a week. He closed his eyes as those childhood memories came back, his father removing his belt as the boys waited for their punishment, often quoting from Ezekiel as the boys trembled and waited for the beating to come.

'The soul who sins shall die. The son shall not suffer for the iniquity of the father, nor the father suffer for the iniquity of the son. The righteousness of the righteous shall be upon himself, and the wickedness of the wicked shall be upon himself.'

It didn't matter which of them had been guilty of what they were being punished for. Their father had decreed that they were responsible for keeping each other on the right path, and so if one did wrong, both would be punished. It was intended as a way of bringing them closer together, but Earl was rebellious as a child, hitting back at the strict regime of their household and doing all he could to get into trouble. Fisher grew to hate him for it. He recalled how many beatings he took, how many hits with his father's belt he received because of his brother. Even now, almost forty years later, it still hurt. He closed his eyes and tried to shoo away the hatred. He knew it wasn't his brother's fault. He was a child, and would one day be judged by the almighty for his actions. Even so, the fact that Fisher had been so desperate to please his father, to keep him happy and show that he wanted to follow in his footsteps became difficult in the face of the constant punishments. It was only later when their father was an old man, his lungs ravaged by years of smoking, a broken shell in a hospital bed, did Miles get his reward. He recalled the way his father had taken his hand, the once shovel like appendages now so much skin and bone, so frail, so wasted away. He had looked Miles in the eye, a broken old man close to meeting his maker at last.

'Miles, I want you to take over the church. Look after your brother. He's a good boy but impulsive. Steer him onto the right track. Make sure you continue to preach the good word of God even if those around you try to sway you.'

He recalled looking at the old man, trying to figure out if it was love, pity, or morbid curiosity he felt towards him. He still wasn't sure now, and could only assume it was a combination of all three. Either way, the old man had died soon after, and Miles had set about doing as he had been asked. Taking the church, further spreading the good word of the lord. He wondered if the old man would have been proud of what it had become. The small family run church had become a business juggernaut, a financial goldmine. Worship, it seemed, was incredibly lucrative.

He contemplated the changes the world was going through, how it was now time for him to step up and take charge. This, he realised, was what he had been preparing for his entire life. The apocalypse, the end of days. The event which would shatter society and remind mankind that they were at the mercy of a god who they hadn't believed in or thought to ask mercy of before. Those people would be frightened, and desperate, and would want a conduit. Someone in the middle who they could speak to in the hope that those prayers might be heard. They needed him.

He opened the bible in his hands, looking at the photograph of his late wife. He touched the image, recalling how she was so cruelly taken at such a young age. A brain aneurysm at just thirty. She had gone to bed complaining of a headache and had never woken up. He was devastated, and for the first time had questioned his faith. Later, he would realise it was just the grief which had caused him to have doubts. Taking her had been a part of God's plan, and whatever he had intended for her in the next life was more important that whatever her time on earth would have been spent doing. He understood that now. Death was as much a part of life as living itself was. That lesson was one which he would need to remember in the coming weeks. Sometimes horrible, appalling things had to be done for the greater good. He had to remind himself that he was a servant of God and the things he would be forced to do was no reflection on him as a person, but on the circumstances that had been forced on them.

He kissed his fingers and touched them to the photograph of his wife, then closed the bible and placed it in his bedside drawer. He felt the familiar light butterfly sensation in his stomach which was always there right before he delivered one of his sermons. There were people waiting for him and the message he was to relay, and today, it was an important one. Perhaps the most important he would ever deliver. He cleared his throat, made one last check on his appearance in the mirror then headed downstairs, ready to spread the good word once more.

CHAPTER SEVEN

Branning & Hamada

Unknown Location

Afghanistan

Branning has no idea where he was. His head was hooded, arms tied behind his back and to the chair in which he was now sitting. Aside from the musty smell of the bag which prevented him from observing his surroundings, it was complete sensory deprivation. Anger nibbled away at him at his stupidity for letting Hamada fool him, and he had to force himself to quell it, relying on his training to keep his head, to think clearly and retain his focus. He was sure he was about to be tortured for information then would be murdered, tossed in a ditch somewhere and left to rot. He knew what was expected of him. No matter what they did, no matter what they asked, he would respond in the same way. Name. Number.

Branning. Three-seven-five-nine-two.

He only hoped he was strong enough to hold out. Training to resist interrogation was one thing, actually doing it would be different altogether.

"Take off his hood."

Branning recognised that voice, and the anger which had earlier nibbled at him now took huge gaping bites.

It was Hamada.

White light filled his vision as the hood was removed. He screwed his eyes up against it, then squinted at his surroundings, remembering his training and trying to take it in to secure any advantage to help him to escape. He was in a stone-walled room with a chipped wood table between him and Hamada who sat opposite, the window at his back stuffed with golden sunlight, casting the Afghan native and the two armed men flanking him into partial silhouette.

"How are you feeling?" Hamada asked.

"Branning. Three-seven-five-nine-two."

Hamada smiled and placed his palms on the table. "As always, you misunderstand me."

He barked something in his native tongue and the two men approached the table.

Here it comes, Branning thought as he squirmed against his restraints. This is where it starts.

They were upon him now, and he hoped it would be a quick death which greeted him. To Branning's surprise, the men didn't kill him. Instead, they cut away the restraints tying him to the chair. Branning rubbed his wrists and stared at Hamada as the two men returned to their previous positions.

"What's going on?" Branning said.

"A misunderstanding, I'm afraid. My men had been tracking us for more than a day and believed I was your captive."

"They could have just asked."

"Either way, it would have been necessary to stop you from knowing the location of our headquarters. As you and I know, this is a fragile trust. It was too good an advantage not to take."

"So where the hell are we?"

"A village not far from where we were camping. The name and specific location do not matter."

"Alright," Branning said, still not entirely comfortable. "I suppose the next question is will they help us?"

"There has been some discussion about that," Hamada said. "Some are sympathetic to the current plight. The others see you as a threat which should be eliminated. However, I have convinced them you can be trusted, Branning, so they have agreed to join our cause."

“And you expect me to believe that?”

“It’s the truth. How you choose to deal with that is your decision.”

“How can I be sure I can trust you?”

“Is the fact that you are still breathing not enough, Branning? If I wanted you dead then this conversation would not be happening.”

“Where I come from, this isn’t how we treat our allies.”

“I think we can both agree that this is a unique situation, Branning.”

"Alright, then I suppose I have to thank you or something, is that it?” Branning muttered, awkward at feeling gratitude for a perceived enemy.

"Don’t thank me yet, there is more you need to be made aware of."

"Go on."

"Although we have many good men here willing to fight and die for the cause, some of our bravest and best are not here in the village.”

“Where are they?”

“They were captured during operations before this situation arose. Your military has them detained in a camp close to the outskirts of Baghdad."

"Prisoners of war?"

"Yes. It seems they were sent there for interrogation to find out what they know."

“What does this have to do with us?”

Hamada leaned close, placing his palms on the table top. "We will need them for the upcoming war. These are brave men, fierce warriors who can help us in our cause. This is why you were allowed to survive, Branning. This is what my men need to prove you can be trusted."

Branning shook his head. "I won’t have authority or clearance to free your men. You have to understand, I’m just a grunt. I have no sway."

"I understand that. Even if you did, it wouldn’t matter."

"What do you mean?"

"It seems this camp I speak of has been taken over by our mutual enemy. Not only are my people prisoner, but yours too. As you see, it would be mutually beneficial for us to free our people in order that they can join our cause. Both of us would benefit and it would further strengthen our mutual relationship."

Branning considered it. He knew to go ahead would be crazy. It was borderline treason. He could be court marshalled, sent to prison for the rest of his life or branded a terrorist sympathiser, disgraced by the country he loved. Then he reminded himself that the world was likely too busy to worry about such things.

“Well?” Hamada said.

"It won’t be easy," Branning said with a shake of his head. "Those camps are well fortified to deter attack. There is every chance those in charge will be well integrated now. They will have supplies, weapons, strategic advantage. It would be a suicide mission if these super soldiers are running the show. Having said that, I agree that we could use the manpower. Do you have any information on specifics? Like where this camp is?"

Hamada barked something in his own language at one of the men by the window who responded by leaving the room.

“In my absence, my men have been observing this camp. Gathering information. In the interest of full disclosure, Branning, they were in the process of planning an assault. This will happen with or without you.”

The man Hamada had sent away returned with a map which Hamada spread out on the table. Branning stood and moved around the table to take a closer look. On the map, just outside of Baghdad, was a red dot.

"The camp is here. It looks to be the central hub for these invaders to run their operations in the area. My people have taken great risk to get close enough to acquire reconnaissance. Thanks to them, we have lots of information."

"Go on," Branning said.

Hamada took another sheet of paper from underneath the map. On it was a crude drawing of the base.

"Based on what my men have seen, this is the layout of the facility. The prisoners are being held here, in this building in the centre."

"What are these dots?" Branning asked, suspecting he knew the answer.

"Patrols," Hamada confirmed. "Always two men, always armed. Every day, trucks full of prisoners are delivered to the facility. It is well defended, apart from the south side here, which faces into open land."

"No," Branning said, shaking his head for emphasis.

"That's deliberate. It’s a classic three wall defence scheme. The fourth wall, in this case, this southern facing land, will be filled with landmines. Because it's so open, anyone approaching would be easy to spot during the day. At night it might be possible to navigate if we knew what kind of mines are being used. If they are standard issue anti-personnel mines, we would need to tread very carefully. Those things are hard to detect and don’t take much to set off. Worst case scenario is if they have a combination if different devices. If so then you don’t want to be trying to pick your way through there."

Hamada nodded. "We suspected as much. We have grenades. Our plan was to trigger the mines by exploding them from a distance."

"Then you lose the element of surprise and I don’t think we want to be rolling in there with these people aware of who we are, how many we have and in which direction we're coming. In addition, there is no cover out there."

Branning pointed to the southern wall of the camp. “Look here. The patrols go across this upper wall. There are machine gun emplacements here and here. We would be sitting ducks.”

"Perhaps not," Hamada said, turning towards Branning.

"What do you mean?"

"Perhaps that is what we should do. With such a distraction, a small team could penetrate the camp elsewhere and liberate the prisoners."

"No, that wouldn't work."

"Why not?"

"Suicide mission. Not so much for the small team going in from the north side, but for the guys around the back. No cover, desert exposure, unexploded landmines, and heavy fire from within the camp. It would be a bloodbath."

"There will be death regardless," Hamada grunted. "If this is the only way, then my men are prepared to make such a sacrifice."

"There's been enough blood spilled without adding to it. I won't send these people into a suicide mission. It's not how I work."

"You think with the American mentality, Branning."

"What does that mean?"

"It means you deal in risk, percentages, and the cost of human life, never the end result."

"I don't see that as a bad thing," Branning snapped.

"The point is, the outlook of my men is different. There is no greater honour than for a soldier to die in battle. Tributes are paid by the people who knew him after his death. It is an honourable way to exit this world. There are shrines, memorials, families proud at the sacrifice their loved ones made. Death holds no fear for my men."

"Death is an absolute certainty if they approach from the south. There is no way they would survive. None at all."

"Do you see another way?" Hamada said.

"No," Branning replied.

"Then we have little choice."

"Alright, let's just assume for a second I agree to this, we don't have the resources or the firepower."

Hamada considered the point for a second and then stood. "Come, Branning. Walk with me for a moment. Let us get some air."

Hamada led Branning out of the room and down a grubby corridor furnished with a tired red carpet. He pushed through another door and then they were outside in a courtyard bathed in blazing sunshine. The sudden explosion of heat took Branning's breath away. It was akin to opening the door of a hot oven. He took a moment to take in his surroundings. Homes were scattered in a rough square around the centre of the village where Branning and Hamada now stood. Branning was aware of the cold gaze of the residents burning into him. There were no friendly greetings or welcomes, just flat, hateful expressions. Hamada ignored it, and started towards the opposite side of the square, his sandals kicking up little puffs of dust as he walked. Branning kept pace, keeping a cautious eye on the villagers who were still staring at him.

"As I said earlier, this is the centre of our operations. So far, these invaders have not yet located us due to the remote location of the village. We are deemed too small to be a concern, which is beneficial to us."

Hamada opened the door to another building opposite the one they had just left. Inside was a prayer room. Guards with rifles stood just inside the entrance, and like the people outside, they gave Branning a cold, vacant stare. Hamada strode on, leading Branning down a short corridor and then through another door. Once again they were outside. Chain-link fences lined either side of the short alleyway, behind which on either side were six skinny, snarling Alsatians, which upon seeing the two men jumped up at the steel, snarling and biting, slamming into the wire.

"I didn't think your people liked dogs," Branning said as Hamada strode towards the connecting building.

"We don't, however, they are good for both protection from intruders and to raise the alarm. Otherwise, they are filthy beasts."

They approached a chipped blue door and Hamada turned to face Branning, his eyes bright and alive under the burning gaze of the sun. "This is our weapons storage area. This is everything we have for the coming fight."

Branning nodded, unsure if Hamada was waiting for a verbal response. Just as he was trying to think of something to say, Hamada turned back to the door, unlocked it and pushed it open.

It was gloomy inside, the windowless room illuminated mostly by the light which spilled in through the open door. Dust swam and undulated in the golden wedge of sun which spilled across the threshold. Branning walked inside, allowing his eyes to adjust to the gloom. He had expected to see a few dozen rifles, perhaps a few grenades. Instead, he was greeted with a veritable arsenal. The walls were lined with weapons, clipped into handmade racks. Submachine guns, rifles and shotguns on the longest wall to Branning's left, pistols and hand grenades on the wall opposite the door, and even a dozen or so rocket launchers still in their green military issue cases were stacked in a corner. In the centre of the room were wooden barrels each printed with the name of one of the weapon types and filled with its matching ammunition.

"I see now why you didn’t want me to know how to find this place," Branning said, feeling a chill dance up his back despite the intense heat within the room. "Where did you get this stuff?"

"You're surprised, I can tell," Hamada said, giving Branning a wide grin. "You expected a few cheap rifles and a box or two of grenades, did you not?"

Branning nodded.

"To answer your question, many of the pieces you see in here are sourced from our supporters in Egypt, Syria, and Turkey. Others come from Europe."

"Those rocket launchers are American issued," Branning said, pointing to the green cases in the corner.

"Yes, although much of our weaponry is sourced from private sellers, some is stolen from your American forces."

"How do you get it?" Branning asked, staring at

Hamada, whose eyes were now just twin pinpricks of light in the gloom.

"How do you think?"

"You killed for it?"

"Not specifically. These were taken after unsuccessful attacks by your British and American colleagues. When the fighting is done, our men take whatever they can which will aid our cause. Those rocket launchers you speak of were acquired following a roadside ambush around five miles from here. We suffered heavy losses but were victorious. Those weapons were in the rearmost vehicle in the convoy. A great find."

"And what about the people? The soldiers?"

"Casualties of war, Mr. Branning. Your people would have done the same to us if the opportunity arose."

"These weapons are covered in blood. You can't just ignore it and expect me to be okay with it," Branning spat.

"Don't be so narrow-minded, Branning. We both know the risks involved in taking up fighting for our country. As my father said, if you don't want to fight, then learn how to be a farmer."

"That doesn’t change the fact that good people have died for you to get these weapons."

"And good people were killed trying to acquire them. There is no difference."

"That doesn’t make it right."

"Does it matter?" Hamada asked around another grin. "We can argue about the past all day and night, but it will not help us. All that should make a difference is that the weapons are here now and available for us to use. Where they came from or how they were acquired should make little difference."

"To you, maybe. It makes a hell of a difference to me. That said, you're right. Under the circumstances, we have no other choice."

Hamada said nothing. He stood in the gloom, watching Branning and letting him come to his own conclusions.

“Okay,” Branning said. "Based on the weaponry you have in here, I think we may have a chance of getting into that compound, although I want to spend a little time going over the map and see if there is another way in. How many men do we have access to?"

"Thirty-seven here in the village. There are a further fifteen held in the compound and whatever American troops are also captive."

"And the men you have here, they're weapons trained?"

"Of course. Many since they were old enough to stand. They are every bit as good as your American soldiers."

"What about explosives? Do you have any other than grenades?"

Hamada crossed the room to a spot behind the barrels. Branning followed. On the floor was a wooden crate. Hamada pried off the lid and showed Branning the contents. Inside were a half dozen rusted artillery shells with wires snaking out of the rear. "Explosives as requested. I believe you Americans call them IEDs"

"Jesus, are they safe to handle?"

"I wouldn't recommend touching them unless you have to."

Heeding Hamada's advice, Branning crouched and leaned closer, his nostrils filled with the smell of dry wood and rust. "Are these Russian shells?"

"Yes."

"Where the hell did you get them?"

"You sound surprised, Branning."

"I am."

"As I said, we have many supporters in other countries, although these didn't come directly from Russia to us but via a supporter of our cause."

"Those wires," Branning said as he continued to stare at the shells. "I take it these can be remotely detonated?"

"Yes, although they are far more primitive than the wireless devices your country uses. These need to be triggered by somebody at the other end of the cable. I'm told they are highly unstable and unreliable, but incredibly effective."

"Alright," Branning said as he stood. "What about C4?"

"No, we have nothing like that. This is everything."

"Okay," Branning said, turning towards Hamada. "I think I have an idea about how we can do this."

CHAPTER EIGHT

Joshua & Genaro

The White House

Washington DC, USA

The destruction of civilisation had so far been easy, and Joshua was growing bored. Instead of the intense battle he had expected, the world had died with a whimper and bent to his will without a fight. He walked the bullet-strewn rooms of the White House, its walls gouged, its floors littered with the dead. Nothing within the structure held his interest, the paintings that adorned the walls to him were listless, works painted by creatures of inferior intellect to him. He was beyond that now, above it. His expectations had been to have experienced euphoria, some sense of achievement instead of the emptiness inside him. It wasn't enough. He craved something more. A challenge, a fight. Surely the governments of the world would try some form of retaliation, at least once they had recovered from the shock at the way he had attacked and been successful. He was starting to wonder if the ease of his victory was due to his own superiority or the arrogance of those he opposed for not believing somebody would reach out and take that which they had fought so hard to keep. He didn't like that. Doubt wasn't something he expected to be feeling. He had shown the world he was serious, and yet had been met with silence. No activity. It made him uneasy.

He stared at the portraits of the presidents who had inhabited the White House over the years, and couldn't help but smile at how inferior they were. At how pathetic their lives were. Compared to the power which lived within him and those like him, they were less than nothing. Beyond insignificant. A vision came to him then, one so vivid and powerful he was certain he was seeing the future.

In it, he stood alone on a smoky plateau of rubble. The sky was deep red and heavy with ash and smoke. As far as he could see in all directions were corpses, bodies piled as high as skyscrapers, limbs twisted and intertwined, rivers of blood running between them. It was a cityscape of the dead, an endless urban city of the extinct, lesser species of humanity. That, he realised was what he wanted. To be able to stand in a world that was his. He would have to crush many more cockroaches yet, that was true, but he was finding that they were scurrying out of sight, and until there were more of his forces created he was unable to make the headway he demanded. He thought about the destructive nature of his predecessors, the humanity of old. How they had abused the resources of the planet, how they had, like parasites selfishly ploughed forward in greed and without any thought to consequences. That at least had been resolved. There were consequences now. He was showing the ignorant lesser species just how it felt to be eradicated with disregard.

"Joshua."

Snapped from his vision, he turned to the door. Genaro stood there, hands clasped in front of him.

“What is it?"

"I did some experimentation on the dead to see if my theories about why they were coming back were right."

"And?"

"It was due to the virus as I thought. It has an incredible will to live which takes it far beyond the normal capabilities of the fragile human shell."

"We know this," Joshua said, a hint of irritability in his voice.

"There's more."

"Go on," Joshua replied, showing a real interest for the first time.

"The dead will go on forever until they find a new host, that much we know. What is interesting is what happens if the body breaks down to the point that the virus can no longer drive it on in search of something to transport its seed into."

"Go on."

"With no physical means of movement, the virus instead puts the body into a coma like state and begins to produce massive amounts of stomach gasses. Eventually, the skin ruptures, or, more accurately, explodes."

"And releases the virus into the air," Joshua said with a half-smile.

"Exactly. Think of it in the same way some plants release pollen. This is the same principle."

"How? You were sure the virus wasn't airborne."

"It wasn't."

"But it is now?"

"So it seems."

"Again, I ask, how?"

"I don't know," Genaro said with an exasperated sigh. "My best guess is some form of rapid mutation, although to change traits so quickly is almost unheard of. It's changing all the time. I have never seen such an aggressive sample. It's evolving, just like we are."

Joshua let the words sink in, then walked towards the older man.

"Find out. I want to know if the airborne spores are more infectious than bites and scratches."

"Of course, although I imagine they are. This is a last gasp attempt by the virus to bond with something, to continue its existence."

"Check and let me know. I may have an idea."

"Absolutely, I will come to you as soon as I know more."

"Good. Keep up the good work. You have proved to be a valuable asset. You will reap the rewards for your loyalty."

The doctor lowered his head. "I serve you without question, Joshua. Just as we all do. Whatever you ask of me will be done."

"Then get to it. This could be the answer I'm looking for."

Genaro hesitated. He looked at the floor, then clasped his hands in front of him.

"Was there something else?" Joshua asked.

"Yes, actually there was."

Joshua smiled. "Then speak my old friend, as this world waits for no man."

Genaro cleared his throat. "Our intelligence has informed us of a possible threat to our operation."

"What kind of threat?"

"A man. One who has the knowledge to do us harm."

A shadow of uncertainty, something Genero had never seen before, passed over Joshua's face. "Who is he?"

"A man called Draven. Ri-"

"Richard Draven." Joshua interrupted. "British-born scientist, specialising in behavioural and genetic replication of the animal kingdom. Studied in Cambridge. Father Deceased, married with two children I believe."

"Yes. You know of him?"

"I make it my business to know such things. What of him?"

"He knows of our project. About our kind"

Joshua snorted. "He knows nothing. His research into our gift was both naive and in its infancy. You worry too much, doctor Genaro. There was a reason you were chosen to lead the programme and not him."

"Actually, he was. It was only when he declined to be involved that I was put in charge of the project."

Joshua frowned and paced the room. "How much does he know?"

Genaro shrugged. "Although he only ever published one paper, it was known in the scientific community that his research continued behind closed doors for years. It's conceivable, however unlikely, that he could possess information which could harm us."

"What kind of information?" Joshua said, spinning to face Genero.

"I…I don't know. This is why I have come to you."

"Where is he?"

"We believe he is on an expedition in Mexico, Somewhere in the Yucatan Jungle."

Joshua considered the situation. Although it was unlikely anything could derail his plans, he wasn't prepared to take the risk. "Send a team out there. Find him. Eliminate him."

"Nobody knows where he is. It could be difficult in

light of recent events."

"That is not my concern. Find him."

"Yes, Joshua. It will be done." Genaro made his leave, hurrying down the hall, sidestepping the corpses which still littered the building.

Joshua walked back to the Oval Office, his feet sinking into the plush carpet as he crossed the room to the large window overlooking the White House grounds. It was a scene of utter chaos. Police and army vehicles were abandoned, doors ajar, lights flashing in silent rotations. Bodies lay where they had fallen, or at least, those which hadn't come back to life after being bitten or scratched by the infected. From his vantage point, he could see at least five of those who had come back, all shambling around the lawn in the search for a host. Beyond the low black fences, the city was awash with smoke which billowed into the air from at least a dozen locations. He pushed the window open, and breathed in the smoky air, instantly transported back to the winter he spent in England when he was twelve with his aunt and uncle as they celebrated Guy Fawkes Night. Every fifth of November, the United Kingdom would celebrate the foiled attempt by Fawkes to blow up the Houses of Parliament in London by lighting fires in their gardens and letting off fireworks long into the night. The air then was cold and fresh, tinged with the smoke of thousands of fires. This was similar enough to make him smile. Unlike Fawkes, his plan had not been foiled. It had gone perfectly, and now, rather than the citizens of the world lighting fires in recognition of failure, the world was burning along with those who clung on to their old lives in desperate hopelessness. The human spirit was a strange thing, Joshua thought as he watched one of the shambling things, his black suit shredded where he had lost an arm, white shirt soaked red due to the blood it had spilled. He half fell, half climbed over the low fence surrounding the property and set out in search of a victim, one of the many who were cowering in homes and hoping that if they stayed inside and didn't get involved, it would pass them by and they could return to their normal lives. How wrong they were. They had no concept of the drive, the determination which was fuelled by the thing that had bonded with him to eliminate the threat of the inferior species. And a threat they were, for as much as Joshua's initial victory had come easy, he knew there was much still to do, and there was nothing more dangerous than the human spirit when all seemed lost and options were limited to fight or flight. Many would choose the latter. They would curl up and die, accept their fate and do so with dignity. Others would fight, and with nothing to lose be dangerous foes. People like Richard Draven.

Something rolled in Joshua's stomach, a feeling he had forgotten.

Fear.

Fear of that particular breed of humanity who didn't know when the fight was lost, who didn't know they had no chance to survive, and who didn't believe in giving up until death was upon them. Those were the dangerous ones now. Not the organised governments, nor the armies of police forces. It was the pockets of people - survivors who knew they were fighting for the existence of their species. Although he would never admit it, Joshua was afraid of those people. Because they alone were the only ones who could stop him, and as unlikely as it was, there were always groups who just refused to accept defeat. There were always those who believed there was a chance.

CHAPTER NINE

Draven, Kate & Herman

Arlington Cemetery

Virginia, USA

The closer they got to the Pentagon, the more the tension increased between them. Kate led the way, trying not to ignore the intense stare of Draven, who was glaring at the back of her head. Herman had tried without success to lift the ugly atmosphere by attempting to make conversation with them and had quickly given up. He had instead reverted to staring at the ground as he walked behind, hands thrust in pockets. They had come out of the small scrub of trees and were walking through the Arlington National Cemetery, the landscape of white tombstones stretching into the distance. It was quiet, the steady chatter of birds the only sound as they neared South Washington

Boulevard.

"Not long to go now," Herman said, a strained grin stretching over his lips as he looked from Draven to Kate.

"You left those people to die," Draven snapped, speaking to Kate rather than replying to Herman.

"I told you to drop it."

"How can you be so cold about it. Will you say the same about my family when we get to the Pentagon?"

"I'm doing my job. You need to think of the bigger picture."

"That doesn't help the people we left behind."

Kate stopped and spun towards him, eyes alive with fire. "What did you want me to do? Drag them along with us to have them turned away at the Pentagon gates? Do you think that would help them, to give them false hope then snatch it away? This is a goddamn global crisis and you're skulking around over a few strangers. You need to get a grip. I made you a promise to try and make contact with your family when we get there. At no point did I suggest we could pick up every damn stranger we encounter along the way."

"Those were people. Civilians, the ones we're supposed to be trying to help. They're not some problem for you to sweep under the carpet."

"The best help we can be to everyone is to figure out how to fix this. Like it or not, this is all on you now. You're the best hope we have"

He glared at her, trying to figure out which insult to launch for best effect. She met his gaze, eyes unwavering.

"You got something to say? If so, spit it out."

"How can you be so uncaring?" Draven asked, genuinely dismayed.

"I'm sorry if that's how I come across. Believe me, that's not how it is. I'm just doing the best job I can under the circumstances, and that means following orders."

"Following orders? Someone told you to leave that family alone back there?"

"Don't be so damn smart. You know what I'm talking about. For the record, my orders were to bring you to the Pentagon so my superiors could review our next move, so that's what I intend to do. You might not like it, but that's the way it is. You do whatever you have to in order to deal with that, as long as you stop giving me a hard time about it."

"Hey, uh, I hate to break up the party over there,"

Herman said, "but I think getting inside the Pentagon might be harder than you think."

They followed Herman's gaze and saw that he could well have a point. Ahead of them, the serenity of the cemetery gave way to a glittering snake of stationary vehicles. South Washington Boulevard was at a standstill, abandoned vehicles stretching in both directions for as far as the trio could see. To their right, a quarter of a mile away stood their destination. Unfortunately, in their fear and uncertainty, the public descended upon the building and gathered outside in a frightened mob in their search for answers and reassurance.

"Shit," Kate said, grabbing her phone. "I'll call ahead, tell them we're coming in."

They snaked through the endless line of vehicles, sidestepping people, trying to fight through the crowds to the front.

"I still have no reception," Kate said, staring at her phone in disgust. Draven saw a flicker of uncertainty and caught another glimpse of the real Kate, the one hiding behind the hard exterior shell. He saw someone vulnerable, someone scared who wasn't as confident in her abilities as her demeanour suggested.

"Cell networks must definitely be down," Herman said. "Maybe your people have shut them off to stop the public from sharing info on what's happening."

"Don't be ridiculous," Kate fired back. "Have you any idea of the chaos shutting down telecommunications would cause? It would cripple everyone, governments included."

"You don't need to tell me," Herman replied. "I know a guy who said radio waves could be changed to give people brain cancer, that your governments know how to do it and use it to assassinate spies. It's been regular practice since the fifties by all accounts. You have to be careful these days. D.T.A man, don't trust anybody."

Kate ignored him and led them further into the crowd. Draven hated confined spaces and felt a moment of panic as he pushed deeper into the sweaty mass of people. He looked over his shoulder beyond Herman and felt his stomach somersault as the crowd closed up into the space where they had just occupied. It was easier to get a sense of the level of panic from the middle of the crowd. The fear and desperation were a palpable thing as people shoved and jockeyed for position, most of them unsure what help if any, the government could give them. Some begged and pleaded for help, others were aggressive, demanding answers when there were none to give.

At the front of the crowd, a barricade had been set up behind which stony-faced soldiers stood, fingers poised over trigger guards should anyone overstep their mark. The noise was deafening as those in the crowd tried to make themselves heard. Kate bullied her way to the front and showed her identification to the hulking soldier at the front.

"Kate Goodall, I need to see Bill Watson," she shouted above the noise.

"Step back ma'am. I can’t let anyone in, I.D or no I.D. We’re on lockdown.”

"You don't understand, I was sent here by Marcus Atkins from Homeland Security. You need to let me in, right now. This is important."

“I’m sorry, there’s nothing I can do. I have orders.”

“So do I. Just radio in, tell them my name.”

“I’m sorry. I can’t do anything. Please step back.”

She tried to duck under the barricade, the soldier moving towards her and putting a hand on her shoulder. “Don’t bother, unless you want to get hurt."

"Just make the call. My boss can verify what I’m

saying to you. It's vital I get inside. You're wasting time here. My friends and I need to get in."

The soldier looked beyond her to Draven and Herman. “You two got I.D?”

“They're civilian. You've seen mine, haven't you? I work for the government for Christ's sake.”

“So do a lot of people in this city, lady. As you can see, we have a hell of a situation here. The last thing we need is any more panic. What did you say your name was again?”

“Goodall. Kate Goodall.”

“Alright, well here's what I'll do. I'll try to get word back inside and see if you check out. In the meantime, you go away. If you are who you say you are, we will call you and-”

“Cell networks are down,” Herman said. The soldier glanced at him then back at Kate.

“If you check out, we will call you and have you brought back in. Until then, I'm sorry but I can't help you."

Kate considered arguing but knew it was pointless. The soldier had specific orders and wasn't about to go against them for anyone. She sighed and turned back to Draven and Herman. "This might make your ears ring."

Before Draven could question her on what she meant, she took her weapon from her jacket and fired it into the air, three sharp rapports sending the crowd running for cover. Kate didn't move. Instead, she stood between Draven and Herman who both stared at her open mouthed.

"You might want to put your hands up," she said over her shoulder as the soldiers rushed them. They complied as Kate too held up her hands, tossing her pistol on the ground first.

“This is how you choose to get us inside?" Draven said as the trio were shoved to the ground and cuffed, before being dragged to their feet and frogmarched towards the building.

"We got their attention didn’t we?” she said as they were bundled inside, weapons trained on them.

"I just hope we don’t rot in prison for this."

"Me too."

"What?" Draven said, more than a little alarmed.

"Relax, it will be fine," she said, even managing a smile. “Probably.”

II

They were placed in separate rooms under guard. Draven had seen a full hour pass on the clock on the wall, and all attempts to ask the guard by the door to contact his family were greeted with silence.

He leaned back in his seat, ignoring the growling of his stomach. He was hungry, angry, and tiring of wasting so much time and was about to protest to the guard again when the door opened and a thick set, bald man walked in. A brown moustache sat above cruel pencil line lips, a bulbous nose and cool blue eyes. The man turned and whispered something in the guard's ear, giving Draven a glimpse of the lumpy roll of skin where the back of his head met his neck. The guard un-cuffed Draven, who rubbed his wrists and at the man in the charcoal suit.

"This way Mr. Draven, we don't have much time," the man said, his accent heavy with a Texas twang.

"That's what I've been trying to say to your guard for the last hour. He wouldn't answer me. Someone needs to contact my family back in England and get them somewhere safe."

"Good. Those were his orders. Either way now isn't the time to discuss this. We will do all we can to contact your family and get them to a safe location. In the meantime, you're coming with me. There are some very important people wanting to speak to you."

"What about the people I came in with?"

"They're waiting too."

Draven was led through offices and corridors into the innermost ring of the pentagon. There, he was shown into a large meeting room dominated by a long mahogany table. Herman and Kate were already seated, the space between them intended for him. He wasn't sure if star struck was the correct word, but it served as well as any as he surveyed the other people seated around the table. There, at its head, sat Paul Carter, the President of the United States.

"Mr. Draven," he said as the hulking man who had shown him in took his seat to the president's right. "Please, come in and take a seat. If Miss Goodall is right, you might be the only person in the world right now who can get us out of this crisis."

As a man who always had something to say, it took a lot to leave Draven devoid of words. However, the unexpected turn of events had caught him off guard. On legs which felt a little weak, he walked to his seat between Kate and Herman and sat.

Herman leaned close, whispering in Draven's ear.

"Please, don't tell them you got all the documents from my trailer, okay buddy?"

Draven nodded, thinking there was little danger of him saying anything. Instead, he swallowed and waited to see what the world's most powerful man had to say.

CHAPTER TEN

The skies were black with ash and smoke. Like a plague they spread, burning crops, the dry plants giving more than ample fuel to the flames. The fires illuminated the skies, spreading with frightening speed. Joshua's men went about their tasks without thought, without question. Gasoline was poured, fires started. Those who tried to intervene were tossed into the fires to burn. Fear had grown within the population, as more of Joshua's men were created, every bite, every scratch adding to their numbers. Those who weren't changed were rounded up on flatbed trucks and eighteen-wheelers cramped with people, who huddled and cowered, waiting to see what would happen to them. Some were taken to the work camps. Others diverted to slaughterhouses. There, they were stripped naked and crammed into pens designed for the animals. There was no discrimination. Young, old, male, female. Every race, age, and size were accounted for. Those who protested or tried to fight were murdered in front of the others as a lesson in what disobedience could mean. It was a frightening display of efficiency. Driven by the desire to serve their master, Joshua's men went door to door, house by house, dragging out those inside who were cowering and frightened and burning the buildings as they went. Some were set on fire with people still inside, another visual example to the people that it was in their best interests to comply. Word spread, and soon, the people were waiting on the streets of their own accord. Heads bowed, trembling as they waited to be taken. This was a coordinated plan, one taking place across the globe. It was beyond pandemic levels. The virus was spreading faster than anyone could hope to contain it. Soon enough, the streets were littered with the dead and ran red with blood.

For the bigger cities, Joshua had a unique plan to infect them and further add to his forces. Cargo planes were commandeered and launched, taking off from fifty destinations in unison. Each plane loaded with the infected, bloated, shambling things close to the end of their host's lives. Stomachs stretched and streaked with the strain of the build-up of gasses. Some escaped through the mouth and anus, covering the cargo hold in faeces as the corpses purged to make room for the ever-expanding gasses. The stench was horrific.

The planes flew in over the major cities of the world, aiming at the more densely populated areas. Once in position, the rear cargo doors opened, and the plane began to climb, spilling its payload of bloated flesh out.

They plummeted five thousand feet towards unforgiving steel and concrete. The cities, the people. Each impact of flesh on concrete making the bloated vessels explode, spattering the infected blood far and wide. People were hit, others breathed in the toxic gasses and micro particles of blood. Like a domino effect the change began, an exponential transformation as body after body impacted cars and building, some landing in the streets or on roofs of houses and buildings. For the people who were already terrified, it was unbearable. Some decided there was no hope, and took their own lives. Others took their chances and ran, unsure what was awaiting them or where they could even go. There was no resistance, no fight. Those who had worked as police officers or firemen, doctors or nurses, gave no regard for their professions. They prioritised their own families, their own safety. Calls to emergency services went unanswered, crimes ignored. Humanity had reverted to it's most basic of instincts, that of self-preservation. Joshua's plan had been to break the human spirit, to destroy its desire to resist his plan. So far it had worked.

CHAPTER ELEVEN

Alan & Family

South Washington Boulevard

Washington DC

USA

After he was left stranded by Kate, Draven, and Herman in the woods bordering the cemetery, Alan Pringle had decided to move his family elsewhere. Packing up their tent and distributing their belongings between himself, his wife Anna and their two children, eight-year-old Jack, and six-year-old Megan, Alan first tried the Pentagon, hoping to convince Draven to allow them to go with him as promised. However when they arrived, the crowd had swollen to enormous proportions, and he knew there was no way he could guarantee the safety of his family in a crowd which was becoming agitated and hostile. Armed soldiers and police ringed the building and looked to be just maintaining control, although it was easy to see it was only a whisker away from getting ugly.

Towards the front of the jam of traffic, with a mostly clear road in front of it, stood a pale crème and blue camper van. He didn't hesitate to usher his family into it. The van had been abandoned by its former occupants, the door open, keys still in the ignition. In front of the camper, Alan saw the reason for the abandonment. Two cars looked to have converged on the same space and had tangled, leaving them at an angle across the lane where the camper sat. A chrome bumper sat in the road, along with tiny diamonds of broken glass. However, Alan wasn't looking at the car wreck. He was looking beyond it. With a little careful nudging, he was sure he could get to the road and get his family out of the city. Verifying the van was empty, then ushered his family inside.

"Are you sure we should be doing this?" Anna said, staring at her husband with fearful green eyes. "This is stealing."

"Its fine, honey," Alan grunted, holding the door open for his less conscience conflicted children to climb on board. "We need this. The people who had it have gone. They left it, and now we need to use it."

"But it's not ours," she said, looking at him and hoping for some reassurance.

"We're desperate. Think of the kids. We need to get out of here."

"I'm not so sure," she said, glancing back at the milling crowd around the Pentagon. "Maybe we should wait here and see if we can get some help."

"Like those people in the woods?" he snapped, then took a breath, forcing himself to calm.

Anna looked at him, and he felt guilt. He had made an easy mistake. He had mistaken fear for indecision. "I'm sorry," he said under his breath. "But think of the kids. Doing the right thing hasn't helped us so far. I'm trying to protect our family."

"Where will we go?"

He hadn't thought that far ahead. He was working on instinct alone, driven by the desire to keep them safe. "Somewhere remote. In the mountains maybe. Somewhere where nobody can find us. Somewhere we can sit this whole thing out," he said, hoping to convince himself as well as Anna that he knew what he was talking about.

"I'm scared. If the kids-"

"The kids will be fine, honey. We all will."

"How can you be so sure?"

"I have to be. It's my job. Now please, get in the camper, okay? We need to make a move."

Anna did as he asked. They had been married for fifteen years, and as much as he would like to be able to say it had been a dream union, the truth was they had gone through their fair share of ups and downs. Both of them had taken out frustrations on the other over the years and had separated on three different occasions. It looked like a relationship doomed to fail until Anna had fallen pregnant with Jack. He had been the glue they needed to make them both try harder. When Megan followed two years later, the arguments were behind them. Sure enough, they still had the occasional disagreement about finances or big family decisions - after all, a leopard can't change its spots - but the family unit was strong enough to ride those waves. Love was a word neither of them liked to say, however, they felt it for each other all the same.

Alan climbed into the camper making sure to lock the door. He didn't want anybody to take his new acquisition. Anna sat at the kitchenette table with the children as Alan climbed into the driver's seat. He turned the key in the ignition, grinning when it grumbled to life first time.

"Hold on back there. I need to nudge through this traffic,"

He put the camper into drive, half wishing he'd taken a few minutes to try and roll the vehicles out of their path, then dismissing the idea. Even though he had convinced his wife otherwise, Alan thought there was a good chance the owner of the van was somewhere in the crowd waiting to get into the Pentagon. He hoped the sheer volume of noise around the building mask the sound he was about to make. He thought about what he would do if the owner came back, perhaps started to bang on the windows and demand to be let in. Maybe he would have a family of his own, children who, like him, he was desperate to keep safe.

Kill them. You'd kill them like the last one who tried to harm your family.

Alan pushed the thoughts to the back of his mind. He couldn't deal with that now. He had enough problems of his own without worrying about the theoretical problems of strangers. Besides, if whoever owned the camper was stupid enough to leave it open and unlocked in the middle of such a huge crisis, then they deserved everything they got.

Alan rolled the camper forward, wincing as metal squealed against metal. He teased the accelerator, pushing the converging vehicles aside to make room. He gritted his teeth as the cars scraped the front of the camper, then gunned the accelerator, the camper lurching between the two cars. The rest was easy. He weaved around a pickup, nudged aside a bike, then they were free, the road stretching ahead of them. The relief was a physical thing. It washed over him, and he grinned, unable to help himself. For five miles, they drove without obstruction. He was in the process of trying to decide what to do next and where they could go when a huge explosion rocked the camper. It slewed across the road, tipping onto its side. He could hear the frightened screams of his family as the camper rolled over and over, tossing him out if his seat amid the debris. After what felt like an eternity, the vehicle came to a halt on its side.

Alan lay in the wreckage, hot blood on his face, leg twisted under him. His wrist was alive with pain.

Debris settled.

The steady drip of fluid.

Smoke.

Fire.

The bitter taste of blood in his mouth.

He could hear his wife moaning although he had no idea where she was. More worrying to him was that he couldn’t hear his children. A thought came to him then, one so awful it made his pain seem like a secondary, less important thing.

No seatbelts.

No seatbelts to protect his children from the crash, no seatbelts to stop their fragile bodies from being thrown around the inside of the camper. Desperate, he tried to lift his head and was rewarded with a sharp jolt of agony racing down his spine.

There were other voices now, calling to each other from outside.

Boots crunching on gravel.

White light spilling in as the door was opened.

More voices, the concussion giving him only snatches of words which he couldn’t quite make sense of.

Get this one.

Eve.

Fit for camp.

What about the woman?

One of the kids didn't make it.

What shall we do with the other one?

A gunshot.

A scream from his wife.

He was moving then, hands dragging him into the light of day. Pain exploded, light filled his vision. Then he saw them standing above him. Chiselled faces. Emotionless eyes. Yellow veins pulsing under their skin. He opened his mouth to speak, just a split second before a heavy boot crashed into his skull and knocked him unconscious.

CHAPTER

TWELVE

Meeting Room

The Pentagon

USA

Draven had grown accustomed to being ridiculed by his peers, which made the fact that the president and his cabinet listened to everything he had to say with keen interest as surprising as it was elating. Getting assurances from the President that every effort would be made to contact his family had taken a little of the pressure off him, enabling him to deliver the information required to the most powerful man in the world. He finished speaking and waited, taking a sip of water with a hand that was still shaking.

"Thank you, Mr Draven," the President said. "What I need from you are answers about how we can stop these things. This is becoming a pandemic. They're hitting us on multiple fronts. With them in control of our nuclear arsenal, as far as we can see our options are limited. I hope you can give us something that might bring us hope."

"Yes sir, I can give you my best opinion, but without access to Dr. Genaro, I'm not sure how much help I can be. Anything I tell you now will be theoretical. A best guess, if you will."

"We are all ears, Mr. Draven. It seems you are our sole remaining expert on these things. Anything you can tell us will be helpful."

Draven looked around the table, the surreal nature of the conversation not lost on him. He cleared his throat.

"Actually, sir, I'm not familiar with the men who are doing this. I only learned about them when I was on the flight over from Mexico. What I do know about are the monkeys that the virus was created from."

"What can you tell us about those, Mr. Draven?"

Draven puffed out his cheeks, exhaling slowly as he organised his thoughts. "Well, they behaved much the way you describe these men who have gone rogue. At their most basic level, they are a very aggressive, alpha male dominant species. The healing properties were only the start, just scratching the surface. The real wonder was in the hive mind they possessed."

“Go on,” the President said, leaning closer in his seat.

“After that first expedition where I took a sample of the Tiger monkey, I made two further trips, both observational. I noted that although they existed in significant sized groups, they deferred to one alpha male, much like a pride of lions. The unusual thing is, the alpha wasn’t the biggest or most dominant.”

“I don’t think I follow,” said the man who had retrieved Draven from his holding room. His eyes were cautious as he laid his palms on the table.

“In nature size is king. The biggest and strongest achieve the most success. It's nature’s way of sorting the weak from the strong, and in doing so, extending the survival chances of that species. The Tiger monkeys were different. Their alpha was middle of the pack. He wasn’t big, but even so, the control he had over the others was remarkable. They brought him food, deferred to him, and obeyed his every command without question. I could have spent a lifetime studying those animals if I’d had the money to do it.”

"I’m led to believe there was no mention of this in your report?" the President said.

"No sir," Draven said, taking another sip of water to calm his nerves. "The report I presented to the scientific community was both rushed and based on my initial expedition. I wanted to touch on the key facts with the intention of delivering a follow-up paper at a later date. Of course, circumstances dictated that would never happen. Ridicule, as you might expect, makes a person less willing to share what he has learned."

"Yes," said the man with the roll of fat on his neck that had led Draven to the meeting. "It seems you were ridiculed. In fact, nobody in the science community took you seriously when we made enquiries about you. I wonder if they might have had a point."

"Bill, don't be disrespectful to our guest," the President said.

"No, it's okay," Draven said, staring at the man known as Bill across the table. "You're right, nobody took me seriously. The fact is that you have these men running around displaying the same traits as those monkeys, which means someone in the government did think it was a worthwhile paper. I like to think that is enough to vindicate me or did you bring me here just to give me the tour?"

"Mr. Draven, we're heading off track here," the

President said, "We need a solution to this problem. Do you have any suggestions?"

Draven pursed his lips and drummed his fingers on the expensive oak table.

"Ants."

"Say again?" the President said, a frown appearing for a second on his forehead.

"Ants, sir. When Miss Goodall, picked me up I was studying fire ants in Mexico. Like all species of ants, the majority of the hive are drones, working for a leader, or queen. The queen dictates everything that happens in the hive. She decides which of her colony become workers, which become warriors, and which forage for food. The ants obey without question for the simple reason that their nature dictates that they comply; it's written into their DNA. Does that behaviour sound familiar, sir?"

"Goddamn, it does," the President said. "The reports of these things say they are acting as one, driven on to do whatever they're doing."

"Exactly. This type of behaviour isn't new. It isn't even unique. The vessel is the only real variable that makes it dangerous. My theory is that like ants, these men, these apex soldiers, are driven to do the will of their leader. One sole individual who commands them all."

"So if we wipe him out, the rest will die?" Bill said.

"No, it doesn't work like that. They wouldn't die, the virus is too strong. What it will do is cause chaos. Without their leader, they would be in disarray and wouldn't know what to do. It would give us a chance at least to fight back."

"So we drop a bomb on the White House. We blow it to hell and end this," Bill said.

"I wouldn't do that," Draven cut in.

"Why the hell not?" Bill snapped, put out by the interjection.

"Because I guarantee they will have a failsafe in place. Remember, superior intelligence, ultimate survival machines. You designed them that way, don't make the mistake of assuming they are stupid."

"So what do you suggest?" Bill snapped.

"We need to capture one of them. I need to dissect it. I need to find out something about the virus that we can use against it."

"This isn't a goddamn computer program," Bill grunted.

"Bill," the President said, glancing at his chief of

staff.

"I’m sorry sir, but this is ludicrous. We're wasting time here."

"You brought me here and asked for my help. This is my best suggestion," Draven said.

"But you don’t know."

"Nobody knows."

"So you could be wrong?" Bill countered.

"Of course, I could, but what harm can it do? If you can get one for me to examine, maybe I can figure it out. Maybe I can find an advantage, something we can use to develop a cure. Hell, nature includes them in every other species on this planet, we have to assume this thing is the same. We’re not working on absolutes here. Everything is a maybe."

"Mr. President, listen to this. Assume. Speculate. This man doesn’t know anything."

"So what would you do?" Draven replied. “You seem intent on shooting down everything I suggest, so you must have a better idea. Let’s hear it, ‘Bill’"

"We have the finest military on the-"

"I should have known," Draven said, shaking his head. "You know, there are some things you can’t fix with a gun. This is one of them. As good as your forces are, they won't win. These men are too strong, too fast. Too organised, and based on the way they're expanding, pretty soon there will be too many of them. Warfare isn't the answer. We have to use this thing against itself. You need to destroy it from the inside. To do that, I need a specimen."

Silence enveloped the room. Nobody, even Draven himself, had expected he would have a near argument with the President's chief of staff, and now the atmosphere had grown heavy. All eyes looked to President Carter, who was drumming his index finger on the table top, brow furrowed in thought.

"Alright Mr. Draven, We'll give you your chance to examine one of these things and find a way to stop them."

"Thank you, sir. I can be ready as soon as you can get me a subject."

"We already have one. Two in fact."

Draven glanced at Kate, who was just as surprised as he was.

"Bill, show Mr. Draven and his team to the lab."

"His team, sir?" Bill said with a frown.

"That's right. As of now, he's project leader on this. Make sure he gets whatever he needs to do his job."

"Yes sir," Bill said, his face screwed up into a scowl. "This way, Mr. Draven," He said as he pushed up from the table and walked to a door at the end of the room. Draven, Kate, and Herman followed.

II

Bill Watson, he with the neck roll and bad attitude, led Draven, Herman, and Kate through the network of corridors in the Pentagon to a silver door recessed against the concrete wall on the inner ring of the building. He scanned his hand on the panel at the side and punched in a number on the keypad underneath it.

"Everybody in," Watson said as the door slid open.

They walked into the tiny space and were joined by the bulky Watson.

"Where are we going?" Kate asked.

"Basement," Watson growled as he once again punched in a sequence of numbers on the panel inside the door.

"The Pentagon has a basement?" Draven said, glancing at Bill.

"Sublevels, five of them. Research facilities, also a nuclear fallout shelter if it's needed. It seems you people are now cleared to access them."

"Five sub floors," Herman said as the doors hissed shut and the elevator started to move. "I told you man, governments, and their secrets. I'll bet they have aliens and all kinds of artefacts down here. The Holy Grail. Noah's Ark, maybe even a spaceship or two."

"Is this guy for real?" Watson grunted at Draven, who was spared having to answer by the doors sliding open.

Either due to having watched too many TV shows or maybe just because he had caught a little of Herman's crazy, Draven almost did expect to see a futuristic underground complex, complete with Bigfoot, a UFO, and Elvis. Instead, they were greeted with red carpet, eggshell walls. Pot plants spaced evenly between the half dozen doors which lined each side of the corridor.

"Expecting something else?" Watson said, reading the disappointment on Draven's face.

"No, I'm just surprised there is a subterranean level here, that's all."

"First excavation was back in 89. Deepest level is the fallout shelter. The public think that in the event of an incident, the president would be moved to one of the locations released into public record."

“Wouldn’t that be the case?” Draven asked.

"Those are unstaffed. Decoys to throw off any potential enemies or crazies from trying to get to the important people whilst the rest of the peasants die. The real bunker locations are kept secret," Herman said before Bill could answer.

Kate rolled her eyes.

"Actually, he’s right," Bill said. "It's unlikely we would ever use one of those locations. Greenbrier, Raven Rock, Cheyenne Mountain, pretty much anywhere you could search for on the internet would be left to house dignitaries, politicians and the like."

"Whilst the man on the street is left to die," Draven grunted.

"You should know it's impossible to save everyone. In the event of a disaster, it's important to retain some infrastructure," Bill snapped. “That means that people of power, people who are influential and can help in the rebuilding of the world. It’s just the way it has to be. Not my call, nor is it my point to argue.”

"And screw everyone else, right? The ordinary people. Jesus, even these men we’re trying to stop are just that. Men. Changed maybe, but humans like us."

"Not just like us. Not in the least. Thanks to your

discovery, they are a huge threat to the security of this country, maybe even the world."

Draven glared at him, his anger masking the fact that he was no physical match for the bigger man if things got ugly. "I had nothing to do with this. If this is why you're being so hostile, you might want to think about directing some of that to Doctor Genaro. I might have discovered it, but he was the one who made it what it is."

"Oh, I blame him too. He might have fired the gun but you supplied him with the bullet."

Draven glanced at Kate and they walked the corridor in silence until they reached the furthest door.

"This is what we're dealing with," Bill said as he opened the door and showed them in.

The laboratory was pristine, white surfaces meticulously polished. Lab equipment was arranged on benches, and computer stations sat idle waiting to be used. None of this was noticed by any of them. Their attention was drawn to the area towards the rear of the lab.

There were two cube-shaped holding tanks, each eight feet by nine, their frames made from reinforced steel. Three sides of the cube were made of bulletproof glass, allowing a full and unobstructed view of its occupants.

Draven forgot all about his companions or arguing with Bill Watson. Nothing mattered to him apart from the occupants of the holding cells. He walked towards them, the scientist in him taking over as he examined the two subjects, making mental notes as he took in the contrasting scenes in each cube. The left-hand occupant was a brute, a huge hulk of a man, yellow tinged veins standing out in stark relief against his muscled torso. He was naked, and his hands were bloody. When he saw them he went into a rage, slamming his fists against the five-inch bulletproof glass and leaving bloody smears in his wake.

"Jesus," Draven whispered as he took a compensatory step back.

"We picked him up just outside of DC. It took twelve men to restrain him. We lost five trying to bring him in." Bill said, keeping his distance.

"You didn't sedate him?"

"We tried. Sedatives don't have much effect on them. We pumped this guy with enough to bring down a bull elephant and he just kept coming. This is calm compared to how he was."

"What's that on his shoulder?" Kate asked, pointing to the jagged wound which was weeping blood.

"Believe it or not, that was a bullet wound. It was down to the bone this time yesterday."

"Regenerative skin?" Draven asked, turning towards Bill.

"You're the expert. It seems that way based on what I'm looking at."

"What about him?" Kate said, pointing to the other cell.

This occupant of this cell didn't scream or shout, or even look at them. He shuffled around the perimeter of the cube, arms at his sides, eyes staring straight ahead through clumpy, listless hair which hung over his face. His pale neck and chest were covered in a thick crust of dried blood.

"What's wrong with him?" Kate whispered.

"We call them shamblers, although the official term is reanimates," Bill said as he joined them at the viewing area.

"What does that mean?"

"This man is dead."

Everyone looked at Bill searching his expression for a lie, then finding none, turned back to the cell. A few days ago, they would have argued that it was impossible. Now they accepted his words as fact. "He was one of ours. In fact, he was part of the team who helped bring that piece of shit in the other cell in. Got himself bit on the neck. He bled out on the street. Confirmed dead. Hell, you could tell just by looking. A few hours later he tears his way out of his body bag in the morgue. Killed four people. Three turned. The other we killed before the virus could take hold. It was a goddamn bloodbath."

"That's impossible. You must have made a mistake, maybe he had a low pulse or something." Draven said.

"No mistake, Mr. Draven. We've known for a few days now. It seems this virus of yours doesn't like its host to die. It reanimates them. Keeps them going until it can pass its little gift onto a fresh body."

"I know some viruses can be potent, others creative in their survival methods, but this is too much. Maybe this man was just in some sort of paralysis or-"

"He bled out, Mr. Draven," Bill said, glaring at the trio. "You won't see it now because of all the dried blood on his neck, but his jugular was severed. His head is lolling like that because his throat has been cut to the spine. Trust me, this guy was as dead as anyone I've ever seen. Maybe now you see why we're so keen to stop this."

"What you're talking about is impossible. Post-mortem reanimation is not achievable."

"Our friend in there says otherwise. Believe me, I wish it weren't true. But the fact is that thing walking around in there was a dead man. Your job is to figure out why and how to stop it."

"Why is he all bloated like that?" Kate asked.

"Ahh, that's another trait of these things. It-"

"Spore sacs." Draven interrupted. "It's readying itself to transfer to a new host."

"Impressive," Bill said, tipping a respectful nod. "You're right. We have reports of these things exploding, and sending this virus of yours into the air. That's not the worst of it, we…." He cleared his throat and looked at his feet, then at Draven. "We have reports of these things being dropped over cities. Seattle, Miami, Chicago, London, Madrid to name a few. Plane loads dropped onto cities and exploding on impact."

"Jesus, the spread of infection would be…. bad," Draven said.

"It is bad. In the space of a few hours, whole cities are being turned. We can't contain it, or control it. I should tell you now, just so we're clear. My recommendation is to begin humane cleansing of the affected areas."

"Humane cleansing?" Draven repeated. "Don't you mean mass murder?"

"Mr. Draven, these people are already dead. We're controlling infection. The CDC agreed before we lost contact with them. This is a threat to our species, not some war over natural resources."

"There will be innocents caught up in the crossfire and you know it. You'll be condemning them. Murdering them. Jesus, you'd be no better than these things we're trying to stop."

"No, you're wrong." Bill snapped. "There will be some collateral damage, granted, but the greater good-"

"Spare me the sermon. It's murder and you know it."

"They'll never know. It will be quick, painless. Better than the alternative." He nodded towards the cells shambling inhabitant.

"You knew about this, these things and what they can do and didn't think to tell the public?" Kate said, glaring at Bill.

"How could they?" Draven said, staring at the swollen shambling thing. "Things are bad enough out there without telling them about this. The first things people would want is answers."

"I agree," Bill said. "More importantly, so does the President. Even if we did want to tell people, we can’t. Communications networks are down. Satellites are unresponsive, the civilian internet is gone. Ours is still active, but internal only. It’s all we have left."

"I don’t understand," Kate said. "Shouldn’t we be overrun with these? The death toll must be in the hundreds of thousands the world over. Why aren’t they all coming back? Why only some of them?"

"That's what we're hoping Mr. Draven here can find out."

“I know the answer to that one,” Draven said, tearing his eyes away from the cell.

“Oh?”

"Natural selection. This virus is a predator, its primary instinct being to ensure its own existence. If the host body is healthy, it's unlikely it would pass its gene on to another host."

"Why wouldn’t it?" Bill asked.

"Competition," Herman said.

"Say again?" Bill snapped.

"Competition. If I was some kind of superman, by

that I mean more than I am already," he said, tipping a wink at Kate, "then I wouldn't want to be passing that on to anything else. You don't want to make rivals for yourself if you don't have to."

"That's right," Draven said. "This is a dominant species, it won't want to make competition for itself."

"You mean our friend here got one right for a change?" Kate said.

"Hey, I'm crazy, not stupid. I'm also a great life partner. You'll find that out for yourself one day," Herman shot back, grinning at Kate.

"No thanks," she said, then turned back to Draven. "So why would this guy be changed at all? The original host is still alive in the cell next door. There was no need to transfer."

"Bill, you said the bite happened when you were trying to capture this thing, right?" Draven said.

"Yeah, it was a hell of a battle."

"And this one on the left, the noisy one, he was shot?"

"Yeah."

"Then that explains it. Look from the point of view of the virus. It's wounded, facing capture. In other words, its own existence is at risk. It's natural to try and pass on its gene to ensure its survival."

"I get it," she said. "It didn't expect to survive."

"Exactly. All it was interested in at that point was ensuring its survival. That's all that matters to them if they are faced with death. At that point, they will do anything."

"Like the kamikaze pilots in World War Two, man," Herman said as he tapped on the glass of the cell. "These things don't give a shit, do they, as long as they spread the love? Reminds me of my cousin Jimmy. He can't keep it in his pants, has like, a zillion kids to different women."

"No, they don't," Draven muttered, again questioning just how many screws Herman had loose. "They do whatever it takes to live. Tenacious, to say the least."

"So how do we stop it?" Bill asked.

All eyes went to Draven. He stared at the two cells, knowing the answer lay somewhere within them, but with no idea how to find it. Like the first chill of late summer, a cold uncertainty crept over him.

"I'm not sure yet," he said. "This is all new information, I need time to process it."

"I've been told to give you whatever you need to get

the job done. We've already taken skin and blood samples from both subjects should you need them. This lab is yours to use."

"Okay," Draven said, shrugging out of his jacket and looking around the room. "What about computer access?"

"Terminals over there in the corner. You're already logged on. As I said before, the civilian internet is down, but you have full access to our private servers for whatever you might need. As you know, the President needs a solution on this now before the public start to ask why the dead are walking the streets and exploding all over the damn place. I'm sure you don't need me to tell you what we're dealing with here. This could be a goddamn pandemic."

"Where are those samples you mentioned?" Draven said. He was already thinking, already processing ideas and theories.

"Cold room, through that door," Bill said. "Whatever else you need, just ask."

"Thanks."

"Let me ask you something straight up, no bullshit," Bill said, staring at Draven

"Shoot."

“Do you think you can stop this? Can you find a way?"

For once Bill was without his usual aggression, and Draven thought he was all the better for it.

"I'll do everything I can. Until I analyse the data, there's no way I can answer that with any certainty."

"It's just... I have a family out there. They weren’t authorised to come here with me. I've sent them out of the city, it’s just..." he swallowed, and lowered his eyes to the floor. "Just please, do the best you can, okay?"

Draven nodded, then looked around the room. "Okay, it’s time we got to work."

CHAPTER THIRTEEN

After the meeting, President Carter returned to his private office, closed the door and poured himself a large scotch. He sank into his seat, enjoying the silence until it was broken by a knock on the door.

"Come," he said as he set the glass of alcohol on the desk.

Watson came into the room, closing the door behind him.

"Take a seat, Bill," the President said with a sigh. "Pour yourself a drink first if you want one. To hell with protocol today."

"I’m fine," Bill said as he sat, folding his hands in his lap.

"Is Mr Draven comfortable in the lab?"

"Yes sir, I've shown him the ropes.”

“You don’t sound too happy about it.”

“It’s not my place to say, Mr. President.”

“Go ahead and spit it out. I have you as my advisor for a reason.”

“Well sir, I’m not convinced we should be relying on Draven to fix this. It’s too big for just one man.”

"What's on your mind?" the President asked.

"Well, I’ll be honest sir, he doesn’t seem so sure. I’m not even convinced he knows what to do. All I keep thinking about is what might happen if he's not the one to help us, about how much time will have been wasted."

"Bill, we've been friends now for, what, twenty years?"

"Yes, sir."

"Have you ever known me to not have a backup plan?"

"All due respect, you weren’t in such a high profile position back then. This is a unique situation."

"Which is all the more reason why I want to have a backup plan in place if this all goes south. I’ll be damned if I’m going to oversee the end of the world."

"What were you thinking, sir?" Bill asked, wishing he had taken up the offer of a drink.

"Based on our limited intel, these things are spreading faster than we can keep up with. We know that."

"Yes, sir, that's right. We're trying to pin them back, but they're strong and well prepared. Plus the infectious nature of them is making battling them close quarters difficult and dangerous."

“Anything from the CDC?”

“No contact, sir. We lost them when the comms networks went down. We do know that there was a sizeable presence of the infected close to the area just before we lost contact. It's a safe assumption they've been compromised.”

"Dammit Bill, I'm not about to sit here and make the same mistakes as my predecessor by sitting on my hands and waiting until it's too late. I would have liked to have some nuclear options, but it seems that option is, for now, off the table. We need something else."

"What did you have in mind, sir?"

Carter hesitated, taking a sip of his drink and setting it on the table.

"Only our missile launch sites are offline, correct?”

“Yes, sir. Even if we could access the sites, the computer systems to control them are inaccessible.

We've been locked out."

"Okay, but that doesn't mean we can't load up some B-52 bombers and go in direct. Really hit these bastards where it hurts."

"Sir, the loss of life would be catastrophic. It's impossible to differentiate civilian and target from the ground. From the air, it would be next to impossible. That was why we resorted to bringing Draven in, to avoid this."

"It's already catastrophic out there, Bill. Jesus, just look at it. I'm presiding over a dying country. And it's not just here. Millions dead in Tokyo, Berlin, and Paris. Half of our forces are fighting blind, the rest are stuck overseas either in similar battles or stranded because they can't get back over here. I thought you were in favour of using force."

"I was, I am, it's just....We have our allies' sir, perhaps they can help us?"

"They have their own problems. Nobody has any spare troops, we're fighting this on multiple fronts. Everyone is. This is unlike anything we've ever had to contend with before. The whole damn world is in disarray. I don't like this idea either, but I don't see an option. Hopefully, we can evacuate most of the major cities in time."

"But sir, with comms down, we couldn’t coordinate an evacuation. We have nowhere to house people, no way of organising it. Hospitals are full or abandoned. We have no safe places, and even if we did, we don’t have supplies. We need food, staff, and security. We don’t have the resources, sir," Bill said, not liking the way the conversation was going.

"You’re right, and that’s why I’m reluctant."

"Reluctant?" Bill said. "You mean you're considering this?"

"The planes are on standby. Two out in the Indian Ocean. There are another couple on the Russian border."

"But sir, you can’t do this without wiping out thousands. It's murder."

Carter slammed his fist on the desk. "You think I don’t know the consequences? This wasn’t an easy call."

"Mr. President, please, this is a mistake. I know I suggested a show of force, but this isn’t the way. Smaller scale, more targeted assaults would be better and lead to less loss of life."

"Relax, Bill. It’s only an option for now. A backup.

With luck, Draven will figure out a way to put a stop to this. But as you said when you came in here, we can't rely on speculation and maybes, and we can't just sit and get our asses kicked without responding."

"When I said we should do something, I didn't mean we should go out there and start dropping bombs on our own cities. Think of how it will make you look."

President Carter grunted, and took a sip of his drink, noting the irony of the role reversal. He had become President Fitzgerald, and Bill had become him, thinking he knew better, thinking the job was easy. Carter had a much greater respect for the recently deceased former commander in chief. He took off his glasses and set them on the desk.

"Bill, the last thing I want to do is put people at risk. God only knows, we've had more than enough death and destruction this last few days. But you have to understand, we can't just sit around here and do nothing. Our forces on the street can't cope, we've lost control of our nuclear missiles and communications are down. The longer we wait the more people die and the more these assholes firm their grip on the world. All I keep thinking is that as bad as the death of thousands would be, surely it's better than hundreds of thousands.

Millions."

"Believe me, I understand your thinking," Bill said. "And for the record, I don't envy the position you're in. But think about this. Think of the backlash. They'll have you for genocide. You'll never see daylight again. We need to give Draven at least a little time to find another option."

"When you came in here, you didn't have so much faith in him," the President grumbled.

"Well, I didn't know this was the alternative."

"I'm not a bad man, Bill," the President said as he finished his drink. "I'm just trying to do the right thing."

At that moment, Bill felt incredibly sorry for his long term friend. It seemed he had aged impossibly in such a short space of time. The job was bigger than Paul Carter had anticipated.

"I know," Bill said with a sigh. "I just don't want you to get into something you can't get out of."

"I think we're already there. I haven't got the slightest idea of how to fix this, Bill. I'm clutching at straws here."

"Nobody does. This isn't just a run of the mill situation. This is a once in a lifetime deal."

"Let’s hope this Draven guy is what we thought and he can find a way to at least give us a fighting chance."

"And what if he can’t?" Bill asked, suspecting he knew the answer.

"Then I'll do what I have to do and face the consequences."

Bill all of a sudden wanted that drink. Not so much for the words the President had said, but because of the utter conviction with which he had said them.

CHAPTER FOURTEEN

THE WHITE HOUSE

WASHINGTON D.C

USA

Genaro walked towards Joshua's office, the hallways lined with his personal guards, the eleven of his original twelve brothers, one of which had already sacrificed himself in bringing down air force one. Despite his new powers, the inner strength he could feel surging through his body, Doubt plagued him. His intention for the programme had been to help the world, to make it a safer place. Never had he expected that his work would be used for such brutal and violent purposes. Although he knew well enough it hasn't been his choice to be a part of it, his stamp was still on it. He imagined J. Robert Oppenheimer and his Manhattan team felt much the same after their work on creating the atomic bomb resulted in the deaths of more than forty thousand people when it was dropped on Hiroshima. He wondered how many deaths had been caused as a result of his own work. How may had the apex virus killed because of its creation? Hundreds of thousands easily, he suspected it would soon be in the millions as Joshua further tightened his grip on the world. The old Genaro would have said something. He would have spoken up for what he believed in, stood his ground and refused to cooperate. That was no longer an option. Like the rest of them, he was a slave, destined to do whatever Joshua demanded no matter how he personally felt about it. For a man who possessed superior intellect to most, the power of independent thinking had been taken from him.

He reached the door to the oval office and stopped, smoothing his suit jacket and preparing his thoughts. This wasn't a report he was looking forward to making. He took a deep breath and opened the door. Joshua was sitting at his desk, palms flat on the table, eyes closed.

Genaro stared at him, a strange combination of love, hate, fear and wonder surging through him. Joshua made no effort to address him, and Genaro knew not to speak first and disturb his master. He waited, counting the seconds in his head. He had almost reached seventy when Joshua spoke, his eyes still closed.

"You have news to report to me, Doctor?"

Genaro cleared his throat. "Yes, Joshua. It's about Richard Draven."

"Go on," Joshua said, still not opening his eyes.

"He isn't in Mexico anymore. He's gone."

"Gone where?"

"The Government sent someone out to get him. He's back on American soil."

"So pick him up here."

"We, can't, Joshua. We don't know where he is."

Joshua opened his eyes, locking his cold gaze on Genaro. "You mean to tell me that the man who could pose a significant threat to us is here in our new home country, yet you can't locate him?"

"I'm sorry Joshua. We're working on locating him. It's likely he's been taken to the pentagon or one of the underground shelters located within the country."

"Likely. Possible." Joshua folded his hands, still not

releasing Genaro from his gaze. "These are words of the old race of humanity. Words laced with excuses, with reasons not to succeed in the missions I give to you. If my own kind are using such words, then how am I expected to lead you into the new world?"

"Joshua, I-"

He exploded into action. He stood, his chair slamming back against the wall. At the same time, he tipped the oak table over, spilling its contents onto the floor. Genaro took a step back as Joshua strode around the table, stopping inches from the older man's face. When he next spoke his words were sinister, a whisper which he knew was enough to get the point across.

"Are you telling me, Doctor Genaro, that you don't expect to locate Richard Draven?"

Genaro stammered, unsure what the right answer was, and realising that he was utterly terrified of Joshua. "No, I mean, we will continue to search, of course, but… I don't know how long it will take to find him."

Joshua glared, and Genaro was sure he was about to be killed for his failure. He was still trying to think of something to say when Joshua went on.

"If Draven is as knowledgeable as you say, and

might be able to help those who would oppose us, then I think the solution is obvious." He turned away from Genaro, skirting around the debris from his turned over table. He walked to the window and stared out at the desolate skyline.

"What kind of solution?" Genaro asked, able to relax now he wasn't being so closely scrutinised.

"A contingency plan. Something to give us leverage if we should need it."

"What did you have in mind?"

Joshua didn't speak at first. He was watching a curling line of black smoke billowing into the air from somewhere in the distance. "If you can't find the man who would oppose us, then bring me those he holds dear."

"Joshua…."

He turned from the window, training his gaze on Genaro. "If you can't find him, then I want his family."

CHAPTER FIFTEEN

Draven, Kate & Herman

Basement Lab

The Pentagon

USA

After seven straight hours in the lab, Draven was aware of two things. First, he was exhausted. Second, he wasn't getting any further in finding out anything new. He looked away from the reams of papers spread in front of him and rubbed his eyes. Kate was adding skin samples to slides for Draven to view under the microscope. Herman was wheeling himself around the room, using his feet to keep the chair in motion as he scribbled away in a notebook. Sensing Draven's eyes on him, He looked up from his scrawling.

"You okay there, man?"

"I'm fine," Draven replied, unable to quite hide a smile. "You having fun?"

"I'm as happy as hell. Have you any idea what my buddies online will think about this when I tell them? Secret underground levels to the Pentagon. Mind blowing stuff."

"You might want to keep that to yourself," Kate said without looking up. "We have alien technology to make you forget."

Herman stopped rolling. "You shitting me?"

"Absolutely not," Kate said, turning towards Herman, a quick flick of the eyes towards Draven saying otherwise. "We have probes. Anal probes."

"Anal?" Herman repeated.

"Oh yeah," Kate said, somehow keeping her face straight. "Barbed, with an end the size of a man's fist. We don't know how it works, just that we shove it up there and just like that. Memory wiped."

Herman cleared his throat. "My contacts, you know, from up there, they never mentioned probes."

"Did you ever ask?" Kate said.

"Well no, but..."

"Maybe you did and you just forgot. Maybe you

already got probed."

“You think so?”

“Oh yeah, it sounds like they didn’t want you to know too much.”

“What about you, man? Do you think she’s right?” Herman said.

Draven wanted to play along, but couldn’t keep a straight face any longer. He grinned, which in turn made Kate laugh.

"That’s not fair," Herman said, “I believed you."

"Sorry, I couldn’t help myself. Seems like a long time since I last laughed," she said.

"I think we all needed that," Draven said. "It's been so damn tense since you came out to Mexico to find me. It's one thing after another."

"How is it coming along?" she asked.

"The research?"

"Yeah."

"Not great, to be honest. I’m struggling. It's like I know what I’m looking for but just can’t seem to see it."

"Take a break, walk around. Give your mind a chance to rest."

"I don’t have time for that. We need a

breakthrough."

"Surely there must be something. Nothing in nature is without weakness," Kate said, a frown crossing her brow.

"That's the problem. This isn't nature. It was made in a lab. It follows its own rules. Someone designed this thing. It's like trying to learn a brand new language from scratch."

"I always remember when Doc Genaro had days like this," Herman said as he started to spin around in slow circles on the office chair. "Mostly early on before he made the breakthrough with Joshua. You should have seen his face when he got it to work. He said he was glad it was Joshua as he always liked him."

"Say that again?" Draven said.

"Doc Genaro," Herman repeated. "He always said he was glad he made the breakthrough with Joshua as he always liked him."

"Herman, this is very important." Draven went on, "did Doctor Genaro specifically refer to Joshua by name."

"Uh, no he didn't."

"What did he refer to him as?"

Herman screwed up his face in concentration, eyes

rolled to the roof as he sifted through his oddly organised brain. "He called him Subject B."

Draven spun in his chair and started to leaf through the documents spread across the desk. "I can’t believe I missed this," he muttered as Kate stood at his shoulder.

"What is it?" she asked.

"All this paperwork, these reports and everything else here is useless."

"Why?"

Because they don't relate to Joshua."

"That's impossible."

"No, it isn’t. For once, I have to agree with Herman and say that the government is keeping a big secret here."

"What kind of secret?" She asked.

"Joshua was the second test subject. There was another before him, someone who was the basis for the human trials that started with Joshua. We need to find out who and where he is right now."

"We need to tell Bill Watson about this," Kate said, standing and heading for the lab door.

"No, not him," Draven said. “I need to speak to the President."

II

Five minutes later, instead of relaying his information to the President, Draven was standing in the hall outside his office, sheets of reports and papers tucked under his arms as Bill Watson said the same thing for the fifth time.

"Mr. Draven, please. Tell me what you need and I'll make sure the President hears the request. He's incredibly busy right now as you can imagine."

"That's not good enough. You're wasting time. He asked for a breakthrough and I have it."

"I was put in charge of this project, Richard. I'm just trying to help."

Bill using Draven's first name didn't fit. It was uncomfortable, like a pair of cheap new shoes. Worse was the half mocking, half empathetic smile on his face. Draven took a deep breath and decided to give Bill just a little snippet, just to let him see the urgency.

"Look, you don't understand the situation. Besides, I remember the President putting me in charge of this project."

"Then tell me," Bill snapped. "If it's as bad as you say, then wasting time arguing in the hallway won't help anyone."

"Okay, fine," Draven said, further developing his growing dislike for the man. "Who was Subject A?"

Bill looked blankly at Draven. "I have no idea what you mean."

"Before Genaro managed to perfect the Apex virus, there was another subject. The one who came first, the basis for the human trials. The notes and paperwork that we have relate to him, not to Joshua like we assumed. I need to know who he was, where he is. He could be the key to this thing."

"How do you know this?"

"Something Herman said made me realise our mistake. If you don't let me speak to the President now to find out who Subject One was, then this whole thing is a waste of time. Now are you going to ask him or am I?"

"Okay, you win. I'll see if he's free." Draven watched as Bill disappeared into the President's office and closed the door. Half a minute later, he returned, poking his plus sized head around the edge of the door. "Come on in."

Draven took a deep breath and followed Bill into the office.

III

"I have no idea," President Carter said after Draven explained the problem.

"With all due respect sir, somebody must know about this."

"I'm sure they do, it's just not me. As you know, my reasons for taking over the presidency were rushed, to say the least. I was only briefed on this ongoing situation. Other projects overseen by my predecessor are as much a mystery to me as they are to you."

"Of course, I understand, sir," Draven said. "Is there any way we could find out? I assume all of President Fitzgerald's staff are still here?"

"Yes, they are. The ones who didn't board Air Force One anyway."

"Is there anyone among them who might have a clue? Anything at all will help, sir."

The President considered for a moment, then turned to Watson. "Bill, who was that man who was working on this? The guy in charge of data analysis for Genaro? I read about him in the briefing report."

"Johnson, sir?"

"No, not him. The other guy. Tall, red hair."

"Martin Hughes?"

"Yes, him. Is he here in the Pentagon?"

"Yes, sir. He's been working a desk job here for the last couple of years. He's up in administration."

"Bring him in here will you? He was involved in this thing at the start. He might know something."

There were no arguments this time. No cocky smiles or trying to build rapport by using the President's first name. This time, Bill Watson did as he was told and hauled ass, striding out of the office to find the desk jockey who could yet be vital to the success of the operation.

"Do you think you can stop this virus, Mr. Draven?" the President asked, eyes cold and confident.

"I'll do my best sir. This is a complex and unique situation. I wouldn't want to suggest anything until I have more information. Everything here is completely reactive."

"Sometimes, the secrecy of projects like this can make following the breadcrumbs difficult. I understand that, Mr. Draven."

Draven was spared from having to fumble around for an answer by Bill striding back into the office with, who Draven assumed, was the mysterious Hughes. The President's description of tall, red hair, was accurate. Hughes stood around six five and was stick thin and pale. His hair was orange - not something he would be able to pass off as strawberry blonde - and his eyes blue and wide, although Draven assumed that could be due to being hauled in front of the President with no notice.

"Come on in," the President said, gesturing to one of the vacant seats on the opposite side of his desk.

The red headed desk worker obliged, firing a mistrustful look at Draven as he took his seat.

"How can I help you, Mr. President?"

"Martin, Mr. Draven here has a few questions. Please answer them as fully as possible. Withhold nothing."

"I'm not sure I know what this is about, sir," Martin said, flicking another glance towards Draven.

"You worked with Dr. Genaro on the Apex project," Draven said.

"For a while," Martin said with a nod. "Doctor Genaro and I didn't see eye to eye, so they moved me on before things got going."

"That's the time I'm interested in. Who was Subject A?"

Martin's Adam’s apple bobbed as he looked from the President to Draven.

“You can answer Martin. Full disclosure.”

"Yes sir,” Martin said, then frowned and swallowed. “I’m sorry but I don’t understand what you’re asking, isn’t Subject A the cause of everything that has happened so far?"

"No. We thought so too, however, it seems the one we're dealing with now, Joshua, is Subject B. As you can imagine, this makes finding Subject A vitally important."

Martin shuffled, his Adam’s apple again dancing to its own beat.

"Are you alright?" Draven asked.

"Yes, sorry, I was just caught by surprise."

"Let me guess, you have no idea where he is?" Draven said.

"Actually, I know exactly where he is. Or at least, where he was."

"Go on," the President said.

"He's in England."

“You’re sure?” Draven asked.

“I’m as sure as I can be. There is no reason for him not to be there.”

The President turned to his chief of staff. "Bill, see if you can get the British Prime Minister on the phone. We need to get a trace on this man and find out where he is."

"Mr. President," Martin cut in, "I'm not sure I made myself clear. I know where he is, as in, a specific location."

"Where is he, Martin?" The President asked.

"Belmarsh Prison, sir."

"You experimented on a prisoner?" Draven said, unable to hide his revulsion.

"Not exactly," Martin said, almost fumbling his words. "He was a civilian, a volunteer. He said he needed the money. We offered to compensate him if he took part. The prison came later, after."

"You're not making any sense," Draven said. "What happened? What did he do to end up in prison?"

"Nothing happened," Martin said with a shrug as he loosened his tie. "He didn't do anything wrong to anyone. For some reason, he just wasn't compatible with the programme."

"Was he given the virus? Did he accept it?"

Martin nodded. "Oh, the bonding went as well as could be expected. It's a very adaptive creation. It was just him. He didn't show the results we were looking for. His body had a natural resistance to the early design."

"A resistance?" Draven said, glancing at the President.

"To the early version of the virus. The later versions of it were more potent and would likely have had the desired effect."

"So why the change?"

"Doctor Genaro was under pressure to get results. He didn't want to wait, couldn't wait and was getting frustrated with Subject A's inability to bond with the virus."

Draven exchanged glances with the President. "So you're saying he was immune to the virus?"

"I don't know. Maybe. I was really just an assistant. We noted a small increase in IQ, but nothing as potent as we were looking for. That's about all I can remember."

"And you didn't think to mention this to anyone?" Bill said.

"It's not like that, I thought you already knew, I mean, why wouldn't you? It was all in Genaro's research. It was nothing to do with me. I was off the project fairly quickly."

"Calm down, Martin. It's fine," the President said. "Nobody is accusing you of anything."

"Wait, this doesn't make sense," Draven said. "How did this Subject One guy find himself in an English prison if he was civilian? Something had to have happened."

Martin cleared his throat and shifted in his seat. "That's why Dr. Genaro and I had our disagreement that led to me moving on. Instead of releasing him from the programme, Genaro wanted to ensure he couldn't tell anyone about the project. He was paranoid and afraid that someone would try to take his research. He didn't want to take that risk, so he gave the order to have him taken and secured."

"You kidnapped him?" Draven said, unable to believe what he was hearing.

"I don't like that word, but, essentially, yes, that's what happened."

"And the British helped?" the President asked, as shocked as Draven.

"They didn't know anything about it. President Fitzgerald made arrangements for them to house what they believed to be a dangerous political prisoner. He was to be kept completely isolated from the rest of the population, no questions asked. A favour to their coalition partners."

"You son of a bitch," Draven said, understanding now why Martin had been so twitchy.

"Look, it wasn't my doing, okay? I fought it every step of the way. The guy was harmless, all he was doing was trying to save some cash to buy a new bike. He wasn't a threat to security or anything else. I even tried to talk to the President, but Genaro beat me to it and told him that Subject One was a potential national security risk and needed to be contained until the research on Joshua was complete. What could I do? I was just a research assistant. I was powerless."

"What did they do to him?" Draven asked.

Martin shrugged. "I guess they had him locked away and forgot about him. Genaro made no effort to free him and the British were doing their neighbours a favour by keeping him there anonymously. It seems to me he must have been lost in the system. In the end, that's why I quit. I couldn't work in those conditions. I can only imagine how bitter he must be by now. All those years on his own."

"Great, so you're saying our only hope of trying to

fix this lies in the hands of a man who has a hell of a grudge against the US government for screwing him over?" Draven grunted.

"This wasn't my fault, sir," Martin said, addressing the President rather than Draven. "I was just part of the team, I did as I was told. As I said, I quit rather than have anything more to do with it. Genaro was obsessed with his work, no matter the cost. There was nothing I could do."

"Mr. President," Draven said, interrupting Martin's pleading. "We need to get that man here. No matter what it takes. He's vital to my ability to try and fix this problem. This could be our shot. This guy could help us to formulate some kind of cure if we can get him here."

"We could talk to the British, see if they would extradite him."

"Mr. President, we don't have time for that. Besides, they have enough problems of their own with this worldwide crisis we're facing. Even getting a hold of someone over there would be near on impossible, not to mention the paperwork we would need to do to make it happen." Bill said.

"It's hit the UK too?" Draven said, feeling a twinge of fear in his gut.

"I'm afraid so," the President said. "Intel is scarce right now since we lost the satellites, but it seems reports of Apex infection are cropping up the world over."

"I didn't realise it was so widespread."

"Make no mistake Mr. Draven. This is a global crisis." Bill said.

"I'll speak to the British Prime Minister," the President said. "We can't afford to wait for paperwork to send this prisoner to us, so I'll be suggesting an unofficial extraction."

"You intend to break him out of an English prison?" Draven said.

"No. We don't have the men available to do it, and even if we could, I wouldn't risk aggravating one of our strongest allies. It will have to be on the Prime Ministers say so, using a team he selects for the job."

"SAS?" Bill asked.

"Probably. I'll ask for the same team who apprehended Joshua in the Boston tunnels. They would be the best option under the circumstances."

"Mr President, it's vitally important we get him out and to us alive. He can't be harmed." Draven said.

"I'll ensure that is made clear, Mr. Draven. Now if

you would all excuse me, I need to speak privately to the Prime Minister in order to arrange this."

Bill led Martin and Draven towards the office door.

"Mr. Draven," the President said, causing all three to turn back towards him. "In the interest of clarity, I should advise you that I can't give you much more time on this. If the extraction fails, if anything happens to compromise this operation, I'll have no alternative but to put a secondary plan into action which doesn't involve you fixing this."

"What does that mean sir?" Draven said, feeling his stomach tighten.

"That means rather than trying to fix this problem, steps will have to be taken to eliminate it. Obviously, I don't want to do that, as it will mean a significant loss of civilian life. This is the last chance I can give you. You need to deliver me something tangible. Our international neighbours are already suggesting nuclear level attacks. I'm sure you are aware of the long-term damage that could cause. I need to give them something concrete to stop them from going ahead."

"I understand sir," Draven said, feeling just a little more pressure. "I'm doing what I can."

"I appreciate that, but you also have to consider the

bigger picture. The world is in disarray. People are frightened. Society as we know it is breaking down. It will only take one incident to trigger World War Three, and I don't want it to happen on my watch."

"All I can tell you, sir, is that I'll do anything I can to fix this. No matter what it takes."

Carter nodded. "That's all I ask, Mr. Draven. I just wanted to ensure you were aware of the situation. Let's just hope the British Prime Minister is willing and able to help us."

CHAPTER SIXTEEN

CHURCH OF HOLY RIGHTEOUSNESS

DALLAS, TEXAS

Earl had come to the realisation that he didn't believe in his brother enough to stay with him and follow his new vision for the church. For years, he had watched the world change into a violent, cruel place that had even made him question his faith and wonder what kind of a god would allow such violence and cruelty to be so widespread. He was also tired. Age was starting to take over, and the simple life he craved was becoming more and more distant thanks to his brother's ever ambitious plans to expand the church into a business juggernaut. Even though the world was such an uncertain place, he was prepared to take his chances rather than stay and watch his brother start some kind of terrorist worshiping cult.

There were few in the house he could trust. The staff was loyal to Miles, so he knew he would have to be discreet when he left. Only Michael knew of his intentions. He was his only friend, the only one he trusted, and although he was saddened by Earl's decision, he at least understood.

Earl finished packing, last placing his bible on top of his clothes then closing the old leather case. As a metaphor for the gulf that had grown between him and his brother, it was a good one. His brother had homes in Miami, London, Spain and France, a fleet of luxury vehicles and businesses funded by the church. Earl owned only the items in his case. The rich lifestyle had never appealed to him. Their father had instilled a simple existence into them as children, taught them humility, something which his brother had forgotten.

There was a knock at his door, and Earl smiled. He had arranged for Michael to come for him once Miles had started his daily sermon. It was the best chance for him to leave unobserved. Earl zipped up the case then crossed the room and opened the door, his smile fading.

Miles stood on the other side, face a careful mix of

disappointment and understanding.

"You're supposed to be delivering your sermon," Earl said.

Miles looked past him to the case on the bed. "I didn't want to believe until I saw with my own eyes."

Earl sighed, knowing there was no way to deny his intentions. "How did you find out?"

"May I come in?" Miles asked.

Earl stepped aside and allowed his brother into the room. Miles entered, and Earl closed the door.

"You haven't changed this room in thirty years."

"It serves my needs. I don't need no expensive luxuries like you do."

Miles walked to the bed and ran his manicured nails across the case. "This used to belong to father."

"It did."

"I didn't realise we still had this."

"It's a good suitcase. Just because it ain't one of those fancy brand names you like, don't mean it's not good."

"I'm disappointed, Earl. I thought we had discussed this."

"I was hopin' to go without a fuss. I ain't stopping you doin' what you wanna do. It's just not for me."

“But he said to them, ‘Do not delay me since the Lord has prospered my way. Send me away that I may go to my master.’”

“Genesis twenty-four fifty-six. I know that one.” Earl said. “Who told you I was leavin’?”

Miles walked to the window and looked out over the lush green landscape. “Michael came to me this morning. He was worried for you. He told me your intention.”

Earl nodded. He shouldn’t be surprised. Sooner or later, everyone fell under his brother’s spell. “Don’t make this difficult for me, Miles. I just wanna go out on my own. Find my own way. This isn’t me anymore.”

“This is our calling, Earl. This is why we are on this earth, waiting for this moment. Why would you abandon me in this time of need?”

“Don’t give me that. I told you before, you can drop the act around me.”

“This is no act. The world is in chaos. I need you, we need you.”

“We?”

“The church. God. Our lord.”

“That’s bull and you know it. This is why I wanted out of here without you knowin’. I knew you’d come in here with your bible quotes and your poison talk. I've had enough of it Miles. I don't want this."

"'This is my commandment, that you love one another as I have loved you. Greater love has no one than this, that someone lay down his life for his friends. You are my friends if you-"

"Do what I command you," Earl cut in, finishing the quote. "John fifteen-twelve. I know that one too. You ain't my god, and you don't command me. These people in the church might have bought what you're selling, Miles. But I don't. You might think you know best, but with what's going on out there in the streets, you're on safer here than anywhere else."

"You sound like a man who has lost his faith."

"And you sound like one who has lost his grip on reality."

Miles shook his head. "Father would be sorry to hear those words come out of your mouth, Earl. To know you had lost your faith would sadden him."

"Me? No, I think you're the one he would be ashamed of. Look at what you've become. You've become a business, the face of a corporate machine. This isn't a church built on faith, but on the dollar."

"You take that back," Miles said.

"Truth hurts, don't it? You've become the thing you preach about, Miles. You've become greed, and lust, and selfishness. I don't want any part of that. I'm glad our daddy ain't here to see what you've become. Now I'm goin' and I ain't coming back. You can say whatever you like, but it won't change a damn thing."

Earl reached out for his case, but Miles got there first, grasping the handle.

"What are you doing, Miles?"

"I prayed for you, Earl. Prayed harder than ever before. I asked for you to be shown the light, to be guided the right way. I hoped he would answer, but with the coming apocalypse, the lord was too busy to listen to prayers for those who have lost their faith."

"Let go of my case, I'm leaving."

"I can't let that happen. I love you, dear brother, more than you realise. But I can't let you just walk out of here. It would be a show of weakness. And weakness is something I can't afford."

"You can't stop me."

"'Father, if you are willing, remove this cup from me. Nevertheless, not my will, but yours, be done.'"

"Enough with the quotes. Just let me go."

"No." miles said, grabbing his brother's frail wrist

with his free hand. "I'm afraid I can't do that."

The two brothers locked eyes and Earl realised that not only was his brother delusional, he was dangerous.

CHAPTER SEVENTEEN

Thamesmead

Greenwich, East London

United Kingdom

Since its opening in the spring of 1991, Belmarsh Prison has become home to some of the most dangerous and violent criminals ever convicted within the United Kingdom. With a capacity of almost a thousand, the prison is sprawled across a series of interconnecting cross-shaped wings comprising a mixture of multi and single occupancy cells.

Following the threat of nuclear attack similar to those which had devastated Tokyo, Paris, and Berlin, a nationwide state of emergency had been called through the entire United Kingdom. Homes and jobs had been abandoned as people fled with their families to places they hoped would be safe. Airports were jammed with citizens hoping to flee the country, only to be told all flights had been grounded until further notice. Those who had decided to stay had discovered that in a matter of hours, currency had lost all sense of value, with food and water becoming the latest must-have commodity. Sporadic riots fuelled by anger and fear sparked at random, further stretching what remained of police forces which were operating on the limit of their skills. Even here, more than five thousand miles away from the perceived epicentre of the disaster, Joshua's men had infiltrated, infecting and murdering in the hundreds of thousands. Like pouring paraffin onto a bonfire, fear and desperation exploded as the death toll rose and the public saw just how powerless the authorities were to combat such a deadly and unique threat. The Royal Air Force had never been so active, with patrols of fighter jets streaking across the skies and reporting back to the Prime Minister, who was in a secure underground bunker just outside of the city limits along with his cabinet and members of the royal family who were present when the attacks began. Two such jets streaked over Greenwich, the high-powered shriek as they thundered on their way rolling down the deserted streets, which were slick with a fine drizzle which had been falling all night, producing an eerie mist which clung to the ground.

Parker noticed neither jet nor rain as he crouched in the dirt, staring at the prison through night vision goggles, casting the imposing building into shades of green.

"Anything?" Trig said, shuffling in a half crouch beside Stanhope.

"No movement. Looks like a fuckin' ghost town." Parker grunted, adjusting the focus controls of the goggles.

"It is. Only people stupid enough to be out on the streets are daft cunts like us, mate."

"Its bollocks," Stanhope chimed in. "The world is goin' tits up and we're breaking into a fuckin' prison. We must be off our trolleys."

"Not just any prison either," Trig said.

"What do you mean?"

"Some nasty fuckers in this place, Stanny. Real bad eggs."

"Like who?"

"Charles Bronson for a start."

"Bronson," Stanhope said, brow furrowing. "I know

about him. Saw him in that film, Death Wish."

"Not that one ya' dozy cunt. Charlie Bronson, you know, violent psycho, been inside more years than he's been out. Likes to strip off and butter himself up then get into fights with the guards. They made a film about him."

"Oh, yeah, I know who you mean now," Stanhope muttered. "Either way, we shouldn't be here."

"This one is direct from the Prime Minister. Doing a favour for the yanks. We need to pull someone out for em sharpish and get him to Heathrow," Parker said, setting aside the binoculars and turning towards the rest of the team. "Problem is, with no satellite info and this bloke we're supposed to extract being lost in the system, it means we're gonna have to go in and search for him."

"Fuck's sake, that could take hours," Trig said, spitting in the dirt for emphasis.

"No, we have an idea where we need to be. Northeast wing. Staff has evacuated, so it should just be prisoners in there for now."

"They just left them in there?" Stanhope said.

"What else were they supposed to do with em mate?" Trig said with a one-sided grin. "Safest place for em' to be. If they're locked up, it will make this job a piece of piss."

"Yeah, well, that's the big if. Depends on if the warden decided to leave em in their cages to die or opened the doors to give em a fair chance."

"What do you think Parker?"

"I don't think it matters to us either way. We've got a job to do and that's all there is to it."

"I know that," Stanhope said. "What I was asking is what you think of this whole thing. It's a fuckin' mess."

"The Yanks seem to be keeping a lot of it under wraps. They know more about it than everyone else which means they probably created the problem. All I know for sure is I've seen stuff this last few days I never thought I'd ever see. Some really fucked up shit I wouldn't have believed if I hadn't seen it for myself. Something somewhere has gone tits up, that's for sure."

"I heard the morgues and hospitals are all full," Trig said, firing a frightened glance towards Stanhope. "Bodies are piling up on the streets. There's nowhere to put them so they just leave em there."

"A mate of mine said they were using football stadiums to hold the bodies. Thousands of em he said. Heard the plan was to set fire to them. Big fuckin' bonfire, like." Stanhope replied. "Some kind of virus going around, somethin' like rabies. Infects you with a bite or scratch, sends you off the rails, does things to you. Fuck that. I'd put a bullet in my brain first."

"It might all be bollocks yet," Parker grunted as he clipped the goggles back onto his belt. "I don't believe anything until I see it for myself. The best thing we can do is deal with the mission. Just like always. This is no different to the stuff we do for our bread and butter every day."

"Did you see what happened to the White House?" Trig said, his voice an octave too high. "Those people, the ones we grabbed in Boston just took it over like it was nothing. They're either brave or stupid."

"Yeah well, we took the fuckers once, so we can do it again if it comes to it. Anyway, none of that matters now," Parker said, standing and pulling his balaclava into position, leaving the bright intensity of his eyes visible. "It's time to go to work."

Stanhope nodded and followed suit, rolling the balaclava down his face and adjusting his weight where he crouched. Trig spat into the dirt and did the same.

"Right ladies," Parker said, flicking the safety off his HK MP5 submachine gun. "Weapons ready. Let's get in and out sharpish."

Stanhope and Trig readied their weapons and followed Parker as he ran in a half crouch across the deserted street and into the prison grounds. Fences and barricades were unmanned. Rubbish skittered across the ground in the breeze. Somewhere far in the distance, police sirens sang their monotonous song as they made their way to yet another emergency. Otherwise, there was silence. They approached the building, a dark tomb against the night sky. The three-man team took cover behind the wall to the entrance barrier; the security office, like the rest of the grounds, empty.

"Looks like the power's out," Stanhope said, his voice muffled by the balaclava.

"Trig, get in there and see if the CCTV is operational. We could do with knowing what we're up against before we head inside."

Like parts of a well-oiled machine, they moved in unison. Parker and Stanhope moved into cover positions, Parker on one knee with his weapon pointing towards the prison, Stanhope covering the street they had just crossed as Trig ducked into the security cabin.

"Power's out, no CCTV," he whispered.

"Alright, let's move on. We follow the plan."

They moved in formation, ducking under the barrier and running towards the main entrance, the imposing rectangular red brick entrance building, which was in complete darkness.

They formed up on either side of the entrance, Trig and Parker on one side, Stanhope on the other. Parker peered through the glass, but could see only shadow draped husks of furniture which betrayed none of the prison's secrets. He unclipped the night vision goggles from his belt and peered through the window, banishing the shadows and allowing him to see inside. Beyond the door, there was a second entrance which was magnetically locked, and beyond a reception desk and waiting area leading into the bulk of the prison. Parker recalled the maps he had studied, the locations of staff rooms, toilets and security station. Satisfied the room was empty, Parker gave the signal to enter. They moved into the prison, pushing the interior reception door open, its magnetic locking function made useless by the lack of power. The team adopted a triangular wedge formation, sweeping their weapons as they scanned the reception area. Satisfied it was secure, they relaxed, lowering their weapons.

"Right, let's secure this unit and prep to move into

the cell blocks. This is our extraction point," Parker said.

"What next," Stanhope said, eyes glimmering in the gloom.

"Through the back there we'll reach the courtyard. On the other side, we're into the prison wings themselves. With luck, it will be clear and the inmates sleeping when we get in. Obviously, without staff to patrol the place, it will be impossible to tell."

"Right, let's crack on then."

Parker nodded and pushed the security door open led them through the free standing metal detectors on the inner part of the reception. Deserted offices led them to another security door with a keypad at the side. Parker punched in the combination and pulled open the door. On the other side was a small courtyard. The three men froze and listened, staring at the smoke rising from the opposite side of the wall accompanied by a dull orange glow of fire. As they listened, they could hear the rowdy sounds of a riot in progress.

"So much for the slow and quiet approach," Stanhope said. "Sounds like they're out of their cages."

"Right, in that case, we move to plan B."

"What's plan B?" Trig asked.

"Forget going though, we go up. Trig, find a way onto the roof. We'll need the rappel lines and explosive charges. Let's move."

The three men set to their tasks as two more fighter jets blasted overhead. Within the prison walls, the rampaging inmates were unaware of their presence.

Trig fired the pneumatic rappel gun, the barbed dart embedding into the brick. With well-practiced efficiency, one by one they ascended, moving in silence as they grouped together on the roof. They moved in perfect formation, eyes wide and aware, weapons ready to fire. This was them at their best doing as they had been trained. Parker led the way, Stanhope second followed by Trig, who of the three was the least experienced but still a deadly killing machine trained to cause maximum damage. They kept to the edge of the roof, away from the adjoining inner yard. They arrived at an air vent, the barred grill thick with dust and oil. Parker raised a fist and dropped to one knee, joined by the rest of the team who formed around him in a rough circle.

There was no need to speak. They had memorised and rehearsed the plan countless times. Each man knew what was expected of him. They removed the vent cover and set it aside, then, attaching rappel lines to the outer frame, lowered themselves into the dusty storage room. Illuminated by the dim pre-dawn light coming through their entry point, the two men took defensive positions, each scanning the room with their weapons. The large storage space was, as per their intelligence information, empty apart from a few dozen dusty boxes of files stacked in a corner, and some broken plastic chairs in the other. The single door ahead of them lead to a short corridor, beyond which another gated door gave onto the prison wing proper where their subject awaited them. They moved on as a singular entity and in complete silence towards the door. Stanhope unhooked the snake inspection camera from his belt. Attached by a thin flexible cable, the camera was used to look underneath doors and examine potential entry points prior to breach. The pictures would be relayed in real time back to the operator's handheld unit. Stanhope activated the device and fed the wire underneath the door.

"Looks clear," he said.

"Let's get it open."

Trig aimed his weapon at the door as Stanhope tried the handle. "Locked," he grunted.

"Pick the bastard," Parker replied.

Doing as instructed, Stanhope took out his lock picking kit, his hands moving with assured ease as he manipulated the tumbler with two thin hooked rods.

"I'm not sure I like this," Stanhope said.

"You saw the prison plans same as we did. This is the only way."

"I know, I still don't like it, though."

"Come on mate, let's just crack on," Trig said

"Remember," Parker whispered. "Lethal force authorised as and when needed. We don't need to be heroes. In and out as quick as we can."

Stanhope nodded and opened the door. The trio filed out, weapons ready. Darkened offices stood silent and abandoned as they moved towards the control room, which was separated from the admin wing by a yellow steel security gate.

Stanhope didn't need to be told what to do. They had gone over and over the plan so many times it was second nature. He jogged ahead and crouched at the gate, taking the PE 7 Explosive and attaching the sticky, putty-like blocks to the door, shaping it to blast out away from them before rigging a detonator. He jogged back, unrolling the wire which he inserted into the detonator control. He looked at Parker, who nodded in response.

The sound was deafening in the confines of the corridor. The gate was thrown off its runner, mangled by the blast. Smoke and dust hung in the air, and yet the three-man team was already on the move, breaching the shredded metal gate and into the command centre. Parker went into the control room, scanning the banks of monitors and controls and located the group lock/unlock function. Only used during an emergency such as a fire or other critical emergency, the controls acted as a master key, unlocking all interior doors and the transitional segments between cell blocks. Parker activated the controls and glanced at the rest of his team as a symphony of unlocking gates greeted them. Unlike the rest of the building, the gates were powered by a secondary generator, ensuring they remained operational in the event of power loss.

"Right, let’s move," he grunted, leading the way as the others fell into formation behind him. There was no more need for silence. Any element of surprise was gone with the blast. They moved deeper into the cell block in search of their target.

II

It had been six years since Ross Jordan had interacted with another human being, unless, he counted the semi-regular visits of the prison guards to bring him his meals or escort him to the exercise yard after everyone else had gone inside. At thirty-eight, he knew his life was waning away in his tiny five by eight cell and was still no wiser as to why. Born in northern Canada to a hardworking middle-class couple, Ross had led a trouble free life, which made the reason for his incarceration - a conundrum to which he still had no answer- all the more puzzling. For as much as it was true that the average prison was full of people who claimed to be innocent, Ross could state hand on heart with absolute sincerity that in his case it was true. He had never broken the law, not even getting as much as a parking ticket. The only questionable thing he had done was taking part in a series of medical trials for the government in an effort to pay for a new motorcycle. The trials were said to be harmless, the doctor in charge, a spindly old guy by the name of Genaro, was insistent the trials were for a good cause, something related to improving the health and wellbeing of the average American citizen. Ross didn't care about that. He was more interested in the hundred dollars a pop he received for letting them take samples of his blood and inject him with whatever shit they were testing. He took part in the programme for five weeks, letting them perform their experiments and taking the cash payment for it, each helping him inch closer to the deposit he needed for his motorcycle when something changed.

He had reported, as always to Genaro's office, a small, stifling room which always smelled of old wood and dust. Genaro greeted him, and Ross saw there was something different about him. He was agitated and tense and kept rubbing at his ear lobe as he paced the office, the usually pristine desk filled with papers and folders containing charts, numbers and hand-scrawled notes. He was rambling, talking gibberish. It was only then he noticed Ross standing there in the office, a look of confusion etched onto his skinny face.

Without warning, Genaro had exploded into a tirade of abuse, shoving Ross out of the door and screaming at him for wasting valuable government time and money. Confused and more than a little shaken up, Ross left, wincing against the winter air as he shoved his hands in his pockets and started to walk, mentally trying to figure out how he was going to fund the purchase of the bike and curious what had bugged Genaro so much, when a black car pulled up alongside him. Three men got out and flashed innocuous identification badges at him. Intimidated by their size and the aggressive nature of their questioning, he barely protested at their insistence he go with them to answer some questions relating to Dr. Genaro's research. He got into the car, realising that something was very wrong about the entire situation.

He was taken to a building somewhere out in the Nevada desert, his questions and protests to the three men in the car going unanswered. Once there, he was handcuffed and locked in a windowless room for three days. No communication of any kind took place. No questions, no explanations. No opportunity to make a call or speak to a lawyer despite him screaming himself hoarse at the door of his cell in demand of answers. On the fourth day, more men in sharp-looking black suits who were different to those who had initially stopped him entered his cell and told him he was under arrest under suspicion of intent to commit terrorism. The accusations were ridiculous, and at the time, he didn't take them at all seriously. He even laughed it off and asked them what evidence they had to convict him. The men in suits declined to answer and told him he would be held in remand until a trial could be arranged. He had asked to speak to a lawyer when he realised the situation was far more serious than he gave it credit for. He was promised a lawyer would be called and made available to discuss the situation with him upon arrival.

It was an arrival which never happened.

Instead, a hood was thrown over his head. He was driven to the airport and bundled onto a private plane and flown halfway around the world to the hellhole he now called home. No lawyers ever came. He was put in the cell he currently resided in with no answers to his questions and no clue what he was doing there. Day after day, he screamed at his door, demanding information, to speak to the American embassy, to someone in charge. Nobody came. Nobody interacted with him. He saw the guards who brought his meals, and others who led him to the exercise yard. Nobody else. The solitude wore him down to the point where he stopped asking, realising that he was never getting out. Someone had put him there deliberately and there was nothing he could do about it. He wasn't even angry, not anymore. His isolation and the slow passage of time had taught him that anger wouldn't help. Instead, he had accepted his fate. It was likely he would, for whatever reason never see the outside of his cell again. It was this level of absolute acceptance of his future which wouldn't let him get up from his bunk when he heard the explosion, nor when the door to his cell slid open. He was convinced it was a trick or a ploy to try and incriminate him and give them another reason to keep him. It was only when the three men clad in black tactical armour appeared at the entrance to his cell did he find the motivation to stand.

"On yer feet, now," one of them snapped, his accent as aggressive as it was English. The three sets of eyes glared at him as he stumbled to his feet.

"Who are you?" he said, the sound of his voice somehow alien to him.

"Shut up," one of them said. "Trig, secure our exit."

The man's colleague responded, jogging off down the corridor.

"What's happening here?" Ross said, suddenly afraid to leave the confines of his cell with these men. The last time he had trusted three individuals, he had been brought to his own private hell.

"Someone wants you out of ere mate," the one who

appeared to be in command said. "And it's our job to do it. Now shut up and come with us."

"Not until you tell me who you are. I'll call the guards."

Parker and Stanhope glanced at each other, then Parker turned back to Ross.

"Do you have any idea what's goin' on out there mate?"

Ross shook his head. "No."

"Hell on Earth mate. Hell on fuckin' Earth. Now move your arse."

Ross moved towards the men, a giddy mixture of nerves and excitement swirling in his gut.

"Right," Parker said, "let's get moving."

The trio stepped into the corridor and moved back the way they had come. As they passed through the haze, Ross took a few seconds to comprehend what he was looking at.

The men who had broken him out of his cell saw it too and reacted immediately. They were shouting, pointing their weapons at the crowd of prisoners who crowded the corridor between them and their way out. The crowd was neither intimidated nor afraid. They had a bargaining chip of their own. At the front of the crowd, with a knife held to his neck, was Trig. His balaclava removed, his nose bloody. Ross watched in sick fascination, wondering how this was about to play out.

"Back up!" Parker grunted, training his weapon on the man who had the knife to Trig's throat.

The man, however, stared right back at Parker, his eyes dull and listless. Death was nothing to fear for these men. They had been condemned and had come to terms that their lives were over.

The man with the knife pressed the blade deeper into Trig's neck, opening a small cut. "You better put those weapons down, cunts, or I'll open this boy of yours up from ear to ear." He grinned as he said it, his mouth a cavern of missing teeth framed by a greying beard.

"I'll put a bullet in you. You'll be dead before you can do it," Parker said, his voice as flat and calm as the knife-wielding inmate.

It was a stalemate. The knife-wielding prisoner didn't react, and continued to stare at Parker, who returned his gaze, his weapon poised ready to fire.

The prisoners name was Leon Kruger, and he was serving a double life sentence for murder after breaking into a house which he thought was empty, only to find its occupants inside. Instead of fleeing, the heroin habit he was doing everything to feed forced his hand. He beat the man to death. The woman he had subjected to a horrific ordeal of rape and torture, before he strangled her and dumped her body next to that of her husband. Their eleven-year-old daughter was asleep in an upstairs bedroom and had awoken with the commotion. Kruger had subjected her to the same fate as her mother. High on his cocktail of drugs, Kruger had left enough evidence at the property to make a conviction easy for the prosecution. Now fourteen years into his sentence, he had killed two fellow prisoners during disagreements, extending his sentence indefinitely and making him one of the most dangerous and feared men imprisoned in Belmarsh.

"I won't warn you again," Parker said as he adjusted the weapon nestled against his shoulder. Stanhope was at his side, staring at the prisoners who filled the hall and blocked their escape route. He counted thirty at least. Many of them armed with makeshift weapons acquired during the riot. Broken wooden chair legs, metal pipes ripped from sinks, knives taken from the kitchen were present. On paper, they were no match for Parker and Stanhope. However, most of them were lifers with no chance of parole, or at least they were before the world had fallen apart. Most of them were no strangers to having guns pointed at them, nor did they seem to care if they lived or died.

"You could call a guard," Kruger said, "But I don't think they're ere mate."

Parker adjusted his weapon, his body tense and rigid, his finger poised over the trigger, ready to act. He looked at Trig, recognising the look in his eye. There was a defiance he knew all too well. It had been trained into them all. Win at all costs, no matter the consequences.

"Shoot him," Trig said, his Adam's apple bobbing against the blade.

"Shut the fuck up, cunt," Kruger said.

As Kruger and Parker stared each other down, Stanhope was still watching Trig. His hand was moving towards his belt. They spoke to each other without words, each knowing what was about to happen.

"Where do you think you're goin' with him?" Kruger said, nodding towards Ross.

Parker didn't answer. Kruger grinned.

"You think we're scared of your guns? You can't get all of us, right lads?" Kruger said.

The other prisoners behind him grunted in agreement.

"We'll rush you. You might take a few of us before we get to you. That's where the fun will really start. We-"

Everything happened at once.

Trig pulled the flash bang grenade from his belt and activated it, rolling it behind him into the throng of prisoners. A non-lethal solution, it was designed to disorientate the enemy, emitting both an explosive sound and blinding flash of light which would incapacitate any potential enemy for up to five seconds. Although designed to cause minimal damage, the weapon's concussive explosion still had a devastating effect in the small confines of the corridor. At the precise time Trig rolled the grenade behind him, Stanhope grabbed Ross and shielded him with his own body.

"Flashbang!" he grunted at Parker, who responded by shielding his eyes as the weapon detonated, the noise deafening. It was all the distraction Parker and his team needed. As the prisoners reeled from the assault on their senses, Parker was already firing his weapon, aiming above the crowd in the hopes of dispersing them and clearing the way.

The prisoners responded, scrambling to get away from the gunfire. It seemed that for all the threatening words of Kruger, they valued their lives more than he did. They retreated back the way they had come, down into the bowels of the prison. It was as the chaos settled that Parker and Stanhope saw Trig on the floor. He was on his side, one hand clutched against his throat and trying to stem the flow of blood which continued to pump between his fingers and spill onto the floor.

"Stanny!" Parker shouted over his shoulder as he scoured the crowd for Kruger, however, he was lost in the pack as they ran back into the depths of the prison. Parker knelt beside rig as Stanhope joined him

"Fucks sake, he's bleeding out," Stanhope said.

"See if you can patch him up, I'll secure the end of the corridor and make sure those fuckers don't come back."

Parker also half hoped to get a glimpse of Kruger and put a bullet in his head.

Stanhope took the medical kit from his belt and set it on the ground, acting on instinct, relying on his training.

"Move your hand Trig, I need to see."

Trig was growing pale. Stanhope leaned in close looking at the thin wound on his neck.

"You might turn out to be a lucky bastard yet Trig," he said, forcing a smile as he took out a roll of bandages. "Doesn't look too deep. Lift your legs up."

Trig did as he was told as Stanhope started to bandage his neck. "Parker. We need to get moving sharpish."

"All clear here," he replied. "Get a move on."

"Come on then Trig, let's be having you." Then, he turned to Ross who was watching from the corner. "You too, let's go."

"I don't think I should," Ross replied.

"Look, mate, because of you, my pal here might die. You either come with and stop moaning, or I'll do something I might regret, no matter who thinks you're so fuckin' valuable. Understood?"

Ross nodded.

"Good, now give me a hand to get him up and out of here."

Ross and Stanhope helped the wounded Trig to where Parker waited. In the distance, they could hear Kruger screaming for their blood.

CHAPTER EIGHTEEN

ALAN AND CAPTIVES
LOCATION UNKNOWN

Alan woke just seconds before the agony of his injuries came back to him. He opened his eye, the left puffy and half-closed, making it next to impossible to see. Beyond the steady rumble of the engine, he could hear someone crying. He was almost certain it was his wife, however, he was face down with his hands tied behind his back, his injured shoulder screaming in protest. He tried to piece together what had happened, the tiny fragments of memory coming together.

The Pentagon.

The camper.

The crash.

His family.

His children.

He tried to turn his head, his nostrils filled with the smell of rust and dirt from the floor of the truck. He could see shadows of people, heads down, arms bound. Some were sitting up, heads lolling with every bounce and jolt of the truck. He mumbled, trying to say his wife's name, but there was something wrong with his mouth. He ran his tongue along his teeth and found several were broken and missing as a result of the crash, and, now that he was aware of them, could feel the steady throb of agony, just one more pain in a world of hurt.

"Agna, agna..." He mumbled, trying to re-learn how to say his wife's name with his broken mouth.

"Shh," a voice close to him said, "Keep it down pal, for your own sake."

"Agna, Agnahh," he said again, swallowing back blood and spit.

"Please, you have to be quiet," a different voice said, this one close to his ear. "They'll kill you."

Alan didn't doubt it. The desperation in the stranger's voice was more than enough to convince him.

"My wifthh," he blurted.

"No women here, this truck is just for the men. Here,

let me help you up."

If Alan had been able to articulate, he might have asked to be left where he was until the pain had subsided, however, he never had a chance, and was dragged into a sitting position, his arms still clasped behind his back. The pain which surged through his body helping him to focus, and he stared through his remaining good eye at his shadowy fellow captives.

"Name's Andy," the man who had helped Alan up said from beside him. He was grimy and had a crust of dried blood on the side of his face which ran into his thinning, curly hair. “You’ve been out for a couple of hours."

"Where isth my wifthh?" Alan slurred around his broken teeth.

"She's not with us. All the women are in the other truck in front."

"Where are we?" Alan said, almost managing to sound normal.

"I’m not sure, we've been out in the wilderness for a few hours now. Well away from civilisation, I’ll tell you that much," Andy said.

"How long hafth they had you capthive?" Alan said, wincing in agony.

"A couple of days. We were one of the first, me and my boy here."

Andy motioned to the figure dozing beside him and Alan felt a wrenching sadness at the loss of his own children. "We were picked up just outside Vancouver. Most of the other people in this truck were picked up along the way. After you, we only picked up a couple more. We've been on the road for a while now."

"Any idhea wthere we're gthoing?" Alan said, struggling to ignore the agony in his shoulder.

"No idea," Andy said with a shrug. "I still don't know what the hell's going on here. Did you hear about the nukes?"

"I did," someone else said on the opposite side of the van, a stocky man with dark skin and a blood-spattered mechanics uniform.

"I did too," someone else added, "just before the TV networks went offline."

"That's when we left," Andy said. "When we heard about the nukes, we just got the hell out of town. A lot of the people in my neighbourhood were holing up in their basements when we got out. Goddamn idiots. As if that would stop a fuckin nuke."

"Did you hear about the guy in charge?" the man in

the overalls said. "The one who took the White House?"

"Yeah," Andy said, placing a protective hand on his sleeping son's shoulder. "Joshua isn't it?"

"Yeah," the man in overalls said. "I've heard some screwed up stories. I heard the British are in full martial law, and others saying the dead ain't staying dead."

"Shut up with that," Andy hissed. "Don't give me that George Romero bullshit. There ain't no zombies out there, just men."

"These ain't just men," Overalls said.

"And how the hell do you know?" Andy asked.

"I shot one. In fact, I shot two, and it didn't do any good. They just keep coming."

"Bullshit," Andy said. "You probably just missed."

"No, man, I didn't miss," overalls said. "I was state shooting champion when I was seventeen. Won it again at eighteen and twenty two. These two I shot were only fifteen, maybe twenty feet away when I pulled my gun. I saw the bullets hit home, I saw them exit and the mess it left. Those bastards still kept walking."

"Shut up man, just shut up. What if my boy hears you?" Andy whispered.

"Maybe he *should* know what we're dealing with. Might be the best way to keep safe."

"I can't put this on him, he's only thirteen. I need to protect him."

"I get that, all I'm saying is... Sorry, what was your name?" overalls asked.

"Andy."

"Andy. I'm Mike. What I'm saying is, it might pay to wise the boy up to this situation. I think we can agree it's gonna get worse before it gets better."

"And what would that achieve? Especially in the situation we're in. Jesus, none of us know where we are, or where we're going. I have to let him keep hope that everything will be alright."

"I get that," Mike said. "And I understand it. You just need to give the kid a fighting chance."

"You know what this reminds me of?" another man said, a podgy, balding individual in a ripped tweed suit and wire-rimmed glasses.

"What?" Andy replied.

"The holocaust. The way this is happening, the way these... people are just maiming and killing at will. Reminds me of the way Hitler treated the Jews."

"And what would you know about it?" Mike said.

"Well, I'm Jewish for starters," the man fired back. "As you can imagine, the attempts to eradicate us from existence is something we tend to be taught about growing up."

As a conversation killer, it worked, and they rode in silence for a while, each of them dealing with the situation in their own unique way.

Mike thought about his daughter and ex-wife, both of which he was trying to get to when he was run off the road and captured. He feared for their safety. His wife was a timid woman, his daughter the same. He was wondering if they were already dead, or worse, had been loaded into a truck the same as the one he was in and were now cowering in the darkness and heading towards a future which was uncertain.

Andy was thinking of his son, and asking himself if he would have the strength to end both of their lives if things got to a point where all hope was lost. He wasn't sure he could, and that scared him more than the chaos of the world falling apart around them.

Apart from his pain, Alan thought about his family, and how he had failed in his efforts to protect them. He made himself a promise, something he would either do or die trying. No matter where they were going, no matter what happened, he would do everything in his power to free his family, even if he himself couldn't go with them. He closed his eyes and leaned his head against the vibrating body of the truck. If anybody saw him crying, they didn't say anything.

II

He dozed, straddling the line between sleep and consciousness. With no sense of time, he had no idea how long they had been driving for apart from the blackness of night had started to lighten into pale shades of grey. A fine rain had started, and through the open back of the truck, he could see a light mist hanging in the trees which lined both sides of the road. The next time he woke, full day had come, allowing him for the first time to clearly see his fellow captives. After what felt like an age, the truck came to a halt. It was then he got a real sense of the fear amongst them. Whatever their fate was to be was about to be revealed.

Boots crunched on gravel as those who had taken them approached the rear of the truck, unlocked the back and dropped it down. One of the two men, both dressed in black fatigues grabbed the man nearest the door by his shirt and dragged him to the ground. Message received, the rest started to file out, grateful to be able to stretch limbs which had been confined to such a small space. Alan and his 'group' were among the last to climb out and see where they had been taken.

It was a farm, or at least it had been. The fences surrounding the property had been built up and wrapped with barbed wire, turning it into a prison. Everywhere Alan looked, people, prisoners just like him, were working. Some were building cabins, others were working on fencing under the scrutiny of the men in black with the red and white skull insignia on their arm.

"It's a damn concentration camp," Andy whispered from somewhere off to Alan’s left.

Nobody tried to correct him, it was true. Alan looked around. Three other trucks pulled in and began to unload their human cargo. The truck containing the women, however, didn’t unload. It drove on towards the second set of gates, which were opened to allow them access. The men followed on foot, trudging through the muddy ground as the drizzle continued to fall.

"Line up there," one of the black-clad men grunted, pointing at a white line spray-painted in the dirt. The men did as they were told, the line becoming five deep and twenty long by the time they were done. Alan was trying to see where the truck containing his wife was going, but he lost sight of it as it made its way up beyond the farmhouse. The man in black stood in front of the frightened men, arms clasped behind his back.

"Citizens of the old world," he barked, his voice rolling through the surrounding trees. "You have been spared the fate of your fellow man to work in the creation of the new world. In return, you will be given food and lodgings and spared from the violence and chaos which flows through the world and will continue to do so until your kind has been erased from the planet."

He began to pace the front line of men. From his position three rows in, Alan could see dull yellow veins glowing under his skin.

"My name is Lucas, and I am in charge of this facility. Make no mistake. This is the safest place for you to be. Out there you face starvation, death, and the constant threat of attack. In here you will be given shelter and food in exchange for your hard work. Any attempt to escape will result in death. Any breach of the rules will result in your death. Any attempt to go against the authority of my men will result in death."

Lucas smiled, a barely perceptible gesture as he

paced in front of the line.

"Forget any notion that someone is coming to help you. They're not. Also, forget any notion you can escape. You can't. The only way you will walk out of this facility is if I choose to let you. You are all now prisoners of a war in which there can only be one winner. The sooner each of you accepts this, the easier your time here will be."

More black-clad troops lined up behind Lucas, all of them stony-faced. Lucas stopped pacing and took his place in front of them. Alan thought this was a routine, something well practiced which he had done countless times in the last days judging by the number of captives he could see working on the farmland. It was a show of strength, a visual representation of their power.

"You will now be assigned into groups and given roles to fulfil. Do them to the best of your ability."

"What if we don't," an anonymous voice said from the back of the crowd.

Lucas hesitated and smiled, then turned and looked out over the people who were working on the grounds of the farm. Some were tending to cattle, others building cabins, others still were digging foundations for more planned constructions. Lucas let his eyes drift over them until they settled on a man who was sawing wood planks for a log cabin which was nearing completion. Filthy and with what looked to be an infected bullet wound in his shoulder, the man was erratic as he worked the saw blade, pausing intermittently to adjust his grip as he gritted his teeth against the pain.

"Him," Lucas said.

One of the men flanking him responded, striding across the boggy land towards the man, who looked up in time to see everyone staring at him. He doubled his efforts and lowered his gaze as the black-clad man approached. Without a word being said, the injured man was grabbed by the arm and dragged across the dirt, somehow managing to keep his feet as he left his saw wobbling in the half cut plank. The man was tossed on the ground in front of Lucas, where he cowered and trembled. Lucas paid him no attention. Instead, he looked at the men standing in front of him. Some looked back, others lowered their heads, not wanting to meet his gaze.

"This man is not making the necessary effort. As a result, he has no use to us. He is a parasite, a waste of resources. Joshua says there can be no freeloaders in the new world. All who wish to be able to live within it must play a part. Now I could shoot this man in the head, right here, right now without fear of consequence and my problem would appear solved, however, I won't. Not through compassion, but because I don't want to waste a bullet."

He jabbed a thumb over his shoulder. "The rest of them are watching. They still work of course, but if you look, you can see them waiting to see what happens. Now instead of killing this man, I could punish him, perhaps strip him of everything. Clothing, dignity, possessions, and then turn him out beyond the gates to let fate decide what happens to him. And yet, to do so means to give him a chance to survive, and in turn rendering such action as a possible reward rather than punishment."

He hesitated again, looking at the men who stood beyond the line in the dirt.

"Or, I could send him back to work, knowing he will give his all because he now knows the possible fates which could await him. With this, I get to keep my workforce, and attain maximum effort from this man where before there was less than fifty percent."

Lucas smiled, and he reminded Alan of some kind of

reptile, maybe a snake. "However, this solution also has its problems, in that it takes away the element of fear, and as you will come to learn, fear is the key to maintaining control. As I'm sure you can imagine, if I were to let this man return to work unpunished, then tomorrow I will have two men slacking from their work, the day after four, then six. It would breed. No, I'm afraid, in this instance, the solution is clear."

Without taking his eyes off the men in front of him, Lucas took out his pistol and shot the cowering man in the back of the head. He made no sound as he crumpled face first into the boggy earth, one filthy foot kicking and scrabbling for a few seconds as the puddle of water around his head turned red. The men who had been brought in gawped open mouthed, as if they were expecting the man to stand again and tell them that this is what could happen to them if they weren't careful, however the man didn't stand, he stayed where he was, one arm tucked underneath him, the other splayed out in the dirt.

"As you can see," Lucas whispered, still wearing his reptilian smile. "In this case, the solution was clear. The price of a bullet was worthwhile in order to maintain the fear amid those who work here. Although I have lost the efforts of this worker, everyone else will have seen this display and will double their efforts, which gives me a much healthier turnover in production, maintains my authority, and rids me of an underperforming worker who didn't appreciate the gift he was given in being allowed to survive. I want each of you to heed this example. Think about it, and learn from it. You are all expendable. If you wish to survive, you do as you are told. It really is as simple as that."

Lucas waited to see if there were any protests, then went on.

"Very good. You will now be assigned your tasks and shown where you will sleep. Prior to that, there is one more vital thing you all should know and pay attention to."

He turned and pointed to the barn which was set away from the farmhouse and heavily guarded by more of the black-clad men, who were in greater number there than anywhere else.

"The barn is restricted. If you approach it, try to access it, or are even heard to be discussing it, you will suffer the same fate as the man lying at your feet. This will be the only warning of this. Understood?"

He waited for a few seconds for a reply, then

nodded. "Good. Then let us delay no further. Prepare to be assigned jobs."

Lucas strode away as the rest of his men started to sort and assign the men into groups. Alan barely noticed. All he wanted to know was where his wife was and what had happened to her.

CHAPTER NINETEEN

Pentagon War Room

Washington DC, USA

Without satellite access, the President of the United States was relying only on the information presented by the network of drones currently in active airspace. Piloted remotely from the ground, the drones were capable of relaying video feed to the war room in the Pentagon. The President and the rest of his staff watched as increasingly disturbing and bleak reports were relayed back, adding to both the tension and workload. The first images were also received of the nuclear attack which had decimated Tokyo, the footage from the drones' high definition cameras showing the immense impact crater surrounded by nothing but flattened earth where the city once stood. Fire and smoke billowed high into the air, drifting for hundreds of miles as the wind carried it away. There was nothing to show a city once stood. No people, cars or structures. Just smoke, fire and death. There was absolute silence in the war room. Every single one of them stared at the footage, unable to comprehend the level of destruction, the devastating loss of life.

"Jesus Christ," The President muttered as he removed his glasses and rubbed his temples. "Any idea on the death toll ?"

"No sir. It's likely to be in the hundreds of thousands at the very least and that's just in Tokyo. We can expect similar numbers from the other locations. This is about as bad as it can get."

"What about on our own soil, are we winning?"

"No sir, I'm afraid we're not."

"What about air support, navy? Anything?"

"Mr. President, everything is in disarray. Every hour that passes we lose more men. We're losing this battle sir."

"How long do we have left?" Carter said, looking away from the horrific drone footage.

"What do you mean sir?" Bill asked.

"How long do we have before Joshua is in full

control?"

Bill cleared his throat and smacked his lips together as he tried to find the words.

"Jesus Bill, just spit it out," Carter snapped.

"Based on their current rate of expansion and the heavy losses we're enduring, I'd say we have a month, maybe less until he has total control. Our infrastructure is severely compromised."

"How the hell did this happen? How did we go from being the supreme power in the world to getting our asses handed to us by a group which we have no knowledge of as far as their intentions went?"

"They were supposed to be ours sir, we never anticipated this could happen."

"What about fail-safes? Backups? What about our intelligence agencies for Christ's sake. The CIA. The FBI. God-damn Homeland Security."

"Homeland is gone, sir. The building was attacked three hours ago. The director, Marcus Atkinson is flying out to the American embassy in India to deal with the crisis in Mumbai and set up a secure base away from the homeland."

Carter leaned on the table and put his head in his hands. "So what options do we have left? We must have something we can do." He looked at the blank faces surrounding him on the table, then realised with dismay it was up to him to decide. He was the one in charge, and it was him who would be held responsible if it all went wrong. He was suddenly less critical of the late President Fitzgerald. He sighed and put his glasses back on. "Bill, is there any way we can make contact with the White House?"

"I believe so. Why?"

"Do it. I want to talk to this Joshua and see if we can negotiate a truce."

"Sir, it's our policy not to negotiate with terrorists."

"Damn it, Bill, do you think I don't know that? I don't know what else you expect me to do. You told me we will be wiped out within the month and that we have no options left. If there's a way to save lives by talking to this guy, then I'm prepared to try."

"What if he doesn't go for it?"

"The way I see it, we won't be any worse off. We have nothing to lose by trying. Get me a secure line and patch it through to my office."

"Sir, are you sure that's wise?"

Carter looked at Watson, then at the strained faces of his staff. Finally, he looked at the screen relaying images from the drones, now showing the charred remains of Tokyo.

"No, I don’t know if it's wise, but it's better than sitting here and doing nothing. Please, Bill. Just get me a line into my office."

"Yes sir," Watson said.

Carter stood and made for his office, closing the doors behind him. He took a moment to enjoy the silence, then strode over to his desk.

Damn you Fitzgerald.

The venom of the thought was a surprise, and yet rather than go away, it grew stronger.

You did this on purpose, he said inside his head as he walked around the oak desk and flopped down into the chair. You knew this was all going to shit then died and left me to pick up the pieces, you stupid old son of a bitch.

Part of it, Carter supposed, was because, for as much as he had been desperate to sit in Fitzgerald’s seat, for as sure as he was he could do a better job and make better decisions, the truth was he was out of his depth. No matter what happened from there on in, he knew his term in office would start under a cloud unless of course the rest of the world imploded under the ruthless arm of Joshua and his destruction of the civilised world, in which case none of it would matter anyway. His brief moment of peace was broken as Bill knocked once and entered the room.

"Do you have him on the line?"

"No, Sir. He insisted on video conference. He wants to see you. It's the only way he would agree."

"Fine, just give me a minute to straighten myself up," Carter said, smoothing down his hair and straightening his tie. There was nothing he could do about the light stubble he had grown, but he supposed personal appearance was the last of his worries. As he readied himself, Bill used the computer in the corner and projected the image onto the flat screen television on the wall of the office showing the navy blue Pentagon screensaver. In the bottom corner, a window cut into the image showing the office and a dishevelled looking President, who despite his best efforts to clean himself up was clearly exhausted.

"Can he hear me yet?" Carter asked.

"No sir, he's on hold."

"Good. Give me a second to get myself together here."

"No problem sir, I need to finish securing the line."

Carter waited as Watson adjusted the image on screen and set up the encrypted line. Eventually, he turned to the President.

"Okay sir, it's ready."

"Okay," Carter said, his heart pounding despite his calm demeanour. "Patch him in, then leave me to speak to him alone."

"Yes sir," Watson said, clicking a button on the computer and making his retreat.

Carter waited and watched as the blue screen faded away and was replaced with a view of his former office in the White House, and his former desk behind which Joshua sat, palms flat on the surface. Unlike Carter, he showed no sign of stress or fatigue. His eyes watched with hungry interest, his mouth hidden behind his beard twisted into an amused smile. His hair was long and hovered just above his shoulders. It wasn't lost to Carter that the man who claimed to be the father of the new world, bore an eerie resemblance to another individual who was the figurehead of religious iconography all over the world.

"You look tired, Mr President," Joshua said, his tone more mocking than sincere.

Carter got straight to the point. "I want to know what

we can do to stop this. You made your point. We need to end the killing."

"My point?" Joshua said, tilting his head.

"You're superior. You can beat us. Isn't that what you wanted?"

Joshua folded his hands on the desk, and Carter realised his words had caused offence.

"You think this is about power or superiority? Did you not listen to anything I said during my last address?"

"Look, let's cut to it here. I want to end this. I'm prepared to do anything to make it happen."

"I see," Joshua said. Carter waited for him to elaborate, and was met with stony silence.

"Did you hear me?" Carter said. "We can end this right now if you tell me what you want." Carter hesitated, having to force the next words out of his mouth. "You can take me if it will end this."

Joshua tilted his head and laughed.

"What's so funny?"

"Mr. President, why would I want you?"

"What do you mean?" Carter replied, ignoring the chill which made the hairs on his arms stand to attention.

"You still don’t understand, do you? You're nothing. A second rate figurehead for a society which will soon be forgotten. Nobody cares about you. Most people are preoccupied with their own battle for survival. No, I’m afraid you giving yourself up won’t be enough."

"Then what will? What can I do to stop this?"

"Nothing," Joshua said. "Absolutely nothing."

"Then we'll fight. We'll do whatever it takes to win," Carter blurted, angry and afraid, more the latter than former.

"I warned you what would happen if you tried to resist," Joshua replied in a near whisper.

"I don’t see what else you can do that you haven’t already."

Joshua leaned closer, eyes alive with fire. "I will destroy this Earth. I will burn every crop. Every tree on this planet will fall. I will slaughter everyone who is of no use to me. All apart from you, Mr. President. You will see the world die. When you stand on a mountain of ashes and look out into the sea of the dead which stretches to the horizon, only then will you be allowed to die."

"Please, there has to be a way to fix this. A compromise."

"No, there is only this way. You insult me by making contact Mr. President. For that, there will be consequences. I don't have the time or inclination to waste my precious hours speaking to such worthless creatures."

"What consequences? What do you mean?"

"Goodbye, Mr. President."

"No, wait-"

Joshua terminated the connection. He sat back in his chair, the one in which the man he was speaking to had never sat. From the back of the room, Genaro stood, arms folded in front of him.

"What are we to do, Joshua?"

"Exactly as I said. Fill the slaughter houses. We will feast on the flesh of man as the world burns."

"We are already ushering people into the slaughterhouses."

"Do more. Pack them in, fill them up. Burn everything else."

"Are you sure this is what you want?"

"Do you doubt me?" Joshua said, giving Genaro the same smile he had shown to the President.

"No, my concern is it might trigger the people into revolt against us. Right now they are confused, they have no outlet and are happy to blame their governments. With this, you would be their target."

Joshua nodded. It was a good point, and yet one with a simple solution. "Then tell them. As the men maim and burn, tell them this is all the doing of President Carter, and he is the one they should thank for the destruction. To ensure this point hits home, I think we need to remind our new President who is in charge."

"What do you need?"

"I want to send him a message. One he can't forget."

II

Carter paced his office, trying to untangle the melting pot of emotions which surged through him. The passionate speech he had planned to deliver to Joshua had never happened due to his own inability to do his job. And that, he realised was the problem. He was sure Fitzgerald would have made a better job of communicating with Joshua and in dealing with the crisis as a whole. It was a sobering feeling to realise that for the years he spent thinking he was the best man for the job, the truth was proving to be different. He argued with himself that he shouldn't judge himself on the current situation, and it was so unique, he could be given a little slack. Another voice, the one he was tending to listen to more and more as the days went by, countered that as President, he should be prepared for anything, no matter how extreme, and the very nature of the job required he be able to handle such things.

The door to his office opened.

"What is it, Bill?"

"We need to move you, sir," Watson said.

"Why?"

"Another nuke has launched. We don't know where it's heading. For precaution, we need to move you somewhere safe."

The President sat in his chair and tossed his glasses on the table.

"Sir, please..."

"Relax, Bill. It's not about to hit here."

"You can't know that sir."

"I do. He told me. The son of a bitch wants me to see this unfold. He wants to punish me for daring to ask him to stop."

"We saw the feed," Watson said. "Either way, it could be a double bluff."

"No, it's not. I know him."

"Sir-"

"Damn it Bill I'm staying here!"

Watson cleared his throat. He had no authority to disobey the President and knew well enough how stubborn a man he was. "Excuse me asking sir, but what should we do?"

"Wrong question, Bill. The right one would be, what *can* we do? "

III

The city of New York was struggling to handle the devastation as

Joshua's men rampaged through the city. Times Square was eerily empty, a landscape of abandoned cars and yellow taxis. Rubbish swirled in lazy cyclones through streets long deserted by the public. The dead littered those same streets, many of them riddled with bullet holes. Others were pulpy, broken messes, trampled during the panic. Some of those who had died, the ones chosen by the virus to continue its existence rose again. The thousands of people who had managed to flee to the safety of the apartment blocks and office buildings looked at the scenes unfolding with shock and disbelief, aware that no help was coming. The reanimates shambled in search of new hosts, oblivious to the wider troubles of the world. Broken limbs hung at their sides, shattered bones exposed under fleshy skin and folds of yellow body fats exposed during whatever horrors they encountered at the end of their living days. For the survivors who were powerless to do anything but watch the foul abominations, there was nothing resembling hope to comfort them. The city was no stranger to such horrors. The much publicised and horrific events of that Tuesday morning in September still resonated with the people who lived worked, and now cowered in fear within the city. Rather than be defeated by the attacks, the citizens of New York came together as one and rebuilt. From the shell of the two buildings which fell at the hands of terrorists, a new structure had arisen. A symbol of hope and determination, a glass and steel construction rising one thousand seven hundred and seventy-six feet into the air, taller than those which preceded it.

As one, they saw it, those people who peered out of their windows still hoping for rescue. For the first time since the attacks, eyes moved from the streets to the sky and the white glow which had appeared. Some cheered and grinned, thinking it was the military at last coming to save them. Others comforted children, pointing to the light in the sky and showing them they didn't need to cry anymore. The joy lasted only for seconds. Smiles melted, children pulled closer to anxious parents as they realised the thing they could see wasn't their saviour, but their coming death. The three hundred and forty kiloton B61 -12 Nuclear Gravity bomb, fired at Joshua's command, streaked towards the heart of the city, where the bulk of its eight million residents cowered in the dark.

Impacting in lower Manhattan, the immense fireball obliterated everything within a two-kilometre radius, those closest to the impact zone unaware of their pulverisation after the brief flash of white light. Those outside of the blast zone saw the immense mushroom cloud roll fifty-two feet into the sky, seconds before the invisible, white hot blast wave shattered windows and burned skin, as the deep roar of the impact rolled through the air. In that instant, over a million people were wiped from existence, reduced to dust. A further two million were injured, many suffering severe burns, or crushed under falling debris. The ensuing fallout of the blast would render New York as an uninhabitable wasteland of flattened, burning earth where the proud city once stood.

As a statement of power and intent, Joshua's message was clear. As word filtered into the Pentagon, President Carter knew without a doubt that the attack was a direct result of his decision to contact Joshua. He had killed those people. Their blood was on his hands. As his staff and generals scrambled around and gathered intel, Paul Carter closed the door to his office, sat at his desk and wept.

CHAPTER TWENTY

PATROL UNIT ALPHA 74B

5 MILES OUTSIDE OF SHARAPOR, INDIA

The car exploded, cascading acrid black smoke into the air and raining debris on the men. Marcus cowered closer to the camouflage military transport as gunfire zinged overhead. It had become apparent that he was not only out of his depth, but the knowledge of warfare he thought he had was completely unlike reality. His experience of it had always come from an air conditioned office through banks of monitors. From there, it was easy to make decisions when his life wasn't at risk. Now, as he cowered amid the roar of automatic gunfire and screaming, he knew the reality of it was different. He looked at the burning husk of the car to his right, the heat taking his breath away. Beside it, one of the soldiers he had been on patrol with lay face down, arm twisted underneath him, blood pooling in the gutter, blue eyes open and staring at the floor. *He was just a boy*, Marcus thought he couldn't have been any more than in his early twenties, and his life had ended in a foreign country at the hands of an unknown enemy. He couldn't remember the soldier's name, and it bothered him greatly. The temptation to scramble over and find out what he was called was high, but his fear and instinct to preserve his own life was greater. The truth was, he didn't belong. He shouldn't be on the frontline. He had used the chaos going on in the world to his advantage on his arrival in India when his only thought was in finding Suvari. He had located the United Nations operation easily enough, and a flash of his Homeland Security identification was enough for them to accept whatever he chose to tell them. He had asked to go on patrol in the hopes of locating her, without understanding the danger he was putting himself in.

Another explosion erupted nearby, bringing down a rain of debris. Broken glass, twisted charred metal. Marcus covered up, waiting for it to stop, then assessed the situation. There had been fifteen of them in two transports when they were ambushed by Joshua's men. Now, just one transport remained and five men including him. He clutched his unfired weapon to his body, too terrified to come out of the protection of the cover the vehicle provided. One of the other soldiers crouched by the front of the vehicle glared at him. "Fucking return fire, we're losing this."

Marcus saw no fear in the man's eyes. No doubt. No uncertainty. He saw a man who knew horror like this, who knew what would be waiting for them when they set out on patrol. Marcus glanced at the man's fatigues and the name printed there.

SETTERFIELD.

Across the street, the other transport was side on across the road, its driver dead and slumped over the wheel, two others in his line of sight also dead where they had been hit. Like Setterfield, the occupants of the transport were returning fire, alternately ducking for cover to reload so one of their colleagues could take over. Setterfield leaned out and fired off an uneven barrage of fire, the noise making Marcus flinch. He watched as empty bullet casing ejected out and littered the ground. Fire was returned, and Setterfield ducked away as the lethal missiles dinged off the armoured bodywork.

“What the fuck is wrong with you? Start firing!” Setterfield screamed as he checked his ammo.

Marcus still couldn’t move. He was frozen in place, knowing that to move meant putting himself in danger and the possibility of dying. Some part of his brain told him that was the likely outcome, and that they were almost certainly going to die and he would never see his wife again. It was that idea which spurred him to action. He scrambled to his knees, still clutching the weapon to his chest. His ears were ringing and skin hot from the heat of the burning car. He risked a peek over the hood, careful to keep his head level with the window frame. The street was in ruins. Buildings spewed flame and smoke, cars were overturned and the street pocked with bullet holes. Bodies of civilian and soldiers alike lay where they had fallen. In front of them, their enemy returned fire from behind an overturned flatbed truck. Marcus ducked and checked his weapon, ensuring it was ready to fire. It was then that the dead solder’s name inexplicably came to him.

Norman.

Keith Norman.

Knowing it didn’t make things any easier, and he

wasn't sure why he made such a big deal of remembering it. Setterfield glared at him again and returned fire around the front of the transport. Marcus was ready, but couldn't bring himself to return fire. He couldn't make himself duck out from behind the safety of his cover and draw attention to himself. Setterfield ducked back behind cover.

"I'm almost out. How much ammo do you have?"

Marcus had plenty but was unable to speak. His ears were ringing with the sounds of war around him.

"Hey, I'm talking to you, how much ammo?" When Marcus again didn't respond, Setterfield peered back around the corner and fired off the last of his rounds, then tossed his gun on the ground. Without hesitating, he took the handgun off his belt and fired off a few more shots. He turned to Marcus again. "If you're not going to fucking use that then give it to –"

Setterfield's face exploded in a cloud of red spray, the warm blood spattering Marcus where he crouched. The soldier fell backwards, another casualty of a war which was looking unwinnable. Marcus stared at him, eyes wide, unable to comprehend what was happening. Everything was overwhelming him. The heat of the fire, the smell of smoke, the taste of blood, the icy grasp of fear in his gut. Across the street, the other soldiers were now down to their handguns. He watched as one, he was sure he was called Corkish, tried to retrieve an automatic weapon from one of his dead colleagues. He ducked out into the street, put a hand on it then was torn apart in a hail of gunfire, falling in a face down half crouch over his fellow soldier.

Marcus stared, trying to combat his instincts and knowing it was pointless to do so. It was then that he did something he would never forgive himself for. He looked at the soldiers who were down to only a handful of bullets , then at his own weapon, which was full and had plenty of spare ammo. He could be the saviour and could give them a fighting chance, but he was no soldier, and fear made his decision easy. Marcus dropped his weapon to the ground, then keeping his head down turned and ran back the way they had come, ignoring the shouts from those he had left behind and praying that one day he would be forgiven for such a cowardly act. The base was just a few miles away and he was sure he could make it. One way or another, his first patrol would be his last. He began to accept the possibility that his wife had not survived, and was by now one of the countless dead who littered the streets.

Part of him thought it was for the best. Even when the sounds of the battle were distant, he wept, knowing that although he had survived, he would have to live with what he had done until the end of his days. He broke into a run, praying he would reach the camp and the safety it provided without those men coming after him and finishing what they started. He only hoped his wife hadn't suffered, and her end had been both quick and painless.

CHAPTER TWENTY ONE

SUVARI & CHILDREN

WALSHET, INDIA

Suvari wasn't sure how long she had been driving. Time had lost any sense of meaning. She stared out of the window at the road ahead, trying not to think about the ordeal she had endured. It was as if she were someone else and detached from her own body. She glanced in the rear view mirror, and immediately averted her gaze. The blood of the men who had raped her, who she had in turn murdered, had dried on her skin. She was in no condition to drive. Despite this, she wouldn't stop. She had let instinct guide her from the city to the less populated outskirts to roads where dense jungle bordered each side and traffic more sporadic.

Her mind was a jumble of thoughts, feelings and questions which had mingled into a thick soup of near panic. She had no idea how to keep the children in her care safe, or if such a thing was even possible with the chaos which had engulfed Mumbai. It was a high likelihood that they would die, all of them, her included. They had no money, no food, and no contact with anyone who might be able to help. She wished Marcus was with her. He would know what to do and would be able to help. She couldn't imagine how he must feel. Despite what people thought, he was an emotional man, and would be frantic with worry until he knew she was safe. She tried the radio again, hoping to hear something other than the hiss of static which had filled the airwaves for the last few hours. Daylight was starting to bleed over the horizon, taking away the cover of night which had allowed them to remain anonymous. She didn't like that. The fewer people she encountered until she made some sort of plan, the better. She looked at her bloody reflection and knew she would need to find somewhere to hide and clean up. They would also need food and shelter. Something caught her eye and she stamped on the brakes, which squealed in protest as the truck slewed to a halt. Ahead was a bus parked across the middle of the road. Its tyres were flat and windows broken. What looked to be dried blood streaked the silver bodywork. Tied between two of the broken window frames was a bloodstained sheet which fluttered in the breeze as Suvari read the message written on it in crude black paint over and over again, trying to make sense of it.

TURN BACK!!!
DEATH AHEAD.
INFECTED ZONE!!!
NOT SAFE!!!

She sat in the truck, engine idling as she stared at the sheet. She had no clue what she was supposed to do. Going back wasn't an option, and now going forward wasn't either. She tried to recall the last vehicle she had seen coming in the opposite direction as she had driven down the pitted dirt road, and couldn't remember. She had been too preoccupied with her thoughts. The bus was either a deterrent or some kind of trap to get people like her to stop for long enough for someone to attack. Fear joined the anxiety in her gut as she imagined hungry eyes watching from the cover of the surrounding jungle. They were completely exposed to any potential attack. Her eyes returned to the message on the sheet.

Death ahead

Infected zone

Something came to her, a memory drifting out of the confusion from when she was in the roadblock in Mumbai with Rakesh. She closed her eyes and was able to experience it again in vivid detail, hoping to verify her feeling that the message on the bus and her memory were linked.

She drew breath and opened her eyes.

Could that be what she had seen? Had the man who had been trying to flee in Mumbai only to be attacked and then stand by his attackers possibly have been killed and then somehow risen again? She wondered if that was what it meant by infected. She laughed a short, sharp bark which was as unnatural sounding as it was inappropriate. The dead coming back to life, rapidly spreading infection. She didn't want to say it. To vocalise the word would make it real, which was something she couldn't face. It was impossible, something reserved for horror novels or late night movies. It wasn't something that could happen. The dead coming back to life. There was a word for it, a word everyone knew, a word which was fun and harmless to say when it was reserved for fiction.

Zombie.

She couldn't say it. Not out loud. Instead, she mouthed it to herself.

Zombie.

Bloody, hollowed out skeletal things with flesh hanging off them, shambling in search of brains.

Zombie.

An army of them, a group walking together through a badly constructed graveyard move set to an ominous musical score as the intrepid heroes found inventive ways to destroy their brains.

Zombie.

That wasn't what she had witnessed. The things she had seen were ordinary people. Not gore covered visual effects tricks. There had been nobody to yell cut or add gallons of fake blood. The people she had seen had been bitten, died, and raised again. Still people, still the same, but different. Changed by whatever surged through their bloodstream. Dead but not. Alive but not really living.

Zombie.

To consider it being able to happen took things to a new level. It would answer the question as to why the world seemed to be falling apart if the dead were somehow coming back to life. It would be impossible to contain, harder to stop. People wouldn't believe, and their ignorance would cost them their lives.

Her stomach knotted and she was crippled by the anxiety that had been threatening to overcome her. She felt as if the cab of the truck was closing in on her. Hands shaking, she fumbled the truck into reverse and turned in the road, heading back the way she had come. Far in the distance, she could see an orange glow on the horizon which wasn't the sun rising, but the city of Mumbai as it burned. She had no intention of going back there after the horrors she had seen. She would try her luck elsewhere.

II

The truck ran out of fuel a few miles outside of Shahapur. She let the sputtering vehicle roll close to the edge of the Bhatsa river, turned off the engine and put her head on the steering wheel. Other than the dull rumble of the dam down river which was one of four which supplied water to Mumbai, there was absolute silence. A hazy morning had broken, probing at a stubborn ground mist which lingered from the previous night. She had been thinking about what she was about to do for some time. She knew it had to be done, however, whilst she was driving, there was a convenient excuse to put it off. Now she knew there was no reason to delay any further. She climbed out of the truck and walked to the rear. The children watched her, eyes wide and frightened. She cleared her throat, trying to force the words out from the pit of her stomach. She realised with dismay that they were afraid of her. They had seen what she had done to those men and saw her now as some kind of monster. She wondered if she knew she was trying to help them. An awful thought came then, one in which the children thought she was kidnapping them, taking them to some unknown fate similar to that of the men who had taken her. It was that idea which was the catalyst for her to project the words and speak about what she had done.

"Don’t be afraid of me," she said, looking at each of them and realising how much of a monster she must look still covered in blood. "Do you understand why I had to hurt those men? They wanted to hurt me, and then they would have hurt you. Do you understand?"

They looked at her, eyes blank and still frightened.

"They would have killed us all. I had to stop them. Please understand."

She was greeted with the same blank expression and was trying to figure out a new way to communicate when the trucks arrived, rumbling off the main road and coming to a halt near them. Armed men leapt from the rear pointing their weapons at Suvari who threw her hands into the air.

"On the ground, now!" one of them barked. Too frightened to react, Suvari could only stare at them open-mouthed.

"Down, do it now!" the man repeated, adjusting his aim at her.

She complied, dropping to her knees as the men approached.

"Were you bit? Whose blood is that?" the soldier shouted.

She was too frightened to respond.

"Whose blood?" the man screamed, the barrel of his weapon now inches from her face.

"Not mine, I'm not hurt," she mumbled.

She was pushed face first onto the ground and had

her hands pulled up behind her back. She could hear the children crying but couldn't move her head to see what was happening. She was dragged to her feet and bundled into a waiting truck filled with people, screaming as the door was locked and she was left in the dark.

CHAPTER

TWENTY- TWO

Draven, Kate & Herman

Pentagon Basement lab

Washington, USA

With Genaro's research proving useless until Subject One was found, Draven and Kate were hunched over microscopes analysing blood samples from the two captured subjects hoping to find something to help them. Herman was playing solitaire on one of the vacant computers. All of them aware of the recent attack on New York but too numb to discuss it. The loss of life would be catastrophic. No matter what happened the world was already changed. He was aware that all of them were involved in one of the biggest events in the history of mankind. A life-changing event for the entire human race. Out of nowhere and without warning, the social structure of the world had been destroyed by one man and his warped vision for a new world. In the end, they had decided that some things were easier to ignore rather than deal with, and so they poured their energy into their work.

Although it was wrong under the circumstances, Draven couldn’t help but be impressed by the ruthless nature of the virus.

"The regenerative properties of this organism are incredible," Draven said without looking up from the microscope.

"I agree. You can see why these guys can take bullet hits without bleeding out" Kate muttered, briefly looking up from her scope.

"That’s only the start. Chemical reactions within the body of the subject are also greatly enhanced. Once administered, it sets about boosting the flaws in the human machine. Self-preservation is its aim. Like it or not, this virus is a survivor. Any damage done to the vessel - in this case the human body - is given instant attention. First, the blood clots, then the body generates adrenaline and endorphins to kill the pain. No sooner is the wound inflicted than it starts to heal and the recipient feels nothing. It really is remarkable. Did you see the difference in blood between our two captives?"

"No," Kate said. "I've only seen the blood from our angry guy over there."

"The differences are astounding. They are like different subspecies. When they are in the living death state, the virus is almost in hibernation. It's a transitional phase but at the same time, it's at its most infectious. The virus at that stage is aware that its vessel is damaged beyond repair and is only going to be usable for a short period of time. It focuses on preparing to move on to a new vessel. As a result, the reanimates are incredibly violent and driven to attack at all costs. That's something we might be able to use."

"What are you thinking?" Kate asked.

Draven looked up from his scope. "I'm not sure yet. There is something there, I just don't see it yet. I'm just throwing ideas around, that's all."

"Want me to take a look?"

"Why not? Maybe a fresh outlook will help. There are some vials over there in the fridge."

"I'll get them," Herman said, standing and stretching. "Could do with a break. This solitaire gets intense, man."

"Thanks, I'm sure it does," Draven said, unable to

help but smile. "Samples are marked with the letter B on the vials."

"Got it. Leave it to me." Herman said as he crossed the room.

"So what are you thinking we can do with these samples?" Kate asked.

"Maybe we can reverse engineer it to make the subject weaker rather than stronger. If we can do that, then we might be able to use it against them, although we would have to figure out how to create it in enough volume, then find a way to administer it, which is its own logistical nightmare. I suppose we could-"

Draven was interrupted by the sound of breaking glass. He and Kate spun on their seats towards the noise. Herman was on the ground surrounded by blood and broken glass.

"Are you alright?" Draven asked.

Herman didn't answer, instead, he held his hands out to them, showing where the glass had punctured his skin, mingling his blood with the virus infected samples.

"Shit, Kate, get the first aid kit," Draven said, rushing to Herman and helping him to his feet.

"Shit, shit, shit," Herman muttered. "I tripped over

my damn boot lace. I’m screwed, man, I’m really screwed."

"Shut up a second. We need to clean you up."

Herman and Draven went to the sink, Herman letting the cold water run onto his hands as Draven took some bandages from the first aid box. There was a deep cut on the palm of Herman’s right hand and two smaller superficial cuts near it. Draven looked at it, then at Herman.

“It might not have gone into your bloodstream.”

“You don’t believe that any more than I do,” Herman said. He took his hands out of the flowing water, the wound immediately starting to bleed again.

“Keep it under the water,” Draven said. He glanced at Kate. She had acquired a biohazard mask and was pouring a white powder onto the spilled vials on the floor.

“Just relax, keep it together. We’ll think of a way to fix this,” Draven said.

"It's too late man, it's in my blood," Herman said, his voice high, eyes wide. "We all know I’m screwed. I’ve been listening to you talk about how quickly this thing works."

"Maybe not, maybe we can -"

"It's okay," Herman said, trying to smile and not able to manage it. "Just tell me how long I have before I start to change."

Draven lowered his head, then looked at Herman. "I don’t know. It could be anything from a few minutes to a few hours. Maybe longer because you weren’t bitten. I don't know."

Herman nodded, then looked at the two captives. "You have to put me in there with them."

"No, we can’t do that, they'll kill you," Kate said as she joined them at the sink.

"No, they won't," Draven said, looking Herman dead in the eye. "They won’t hurt their own kind."

“Their own kind?” Kate said, staring at Draven. “You’re giving up on him just like that?”

“Of course not, I don’t want to, but be realistic. There are thousands of people here in this building. We have to consider infection control.”

“You sound so cold. Don’t you feel anything?” she asked, glaring at him

“Look, Kate-”

"It’s okay,” Herman cut in. “It’s for the best. You need to consider your own safety. Lock me up. I don’t want to hurt anyone."

"There must be something we can do," Kate said.

Draven looked at her and shook his head. "He's right. It's safer for everyone if he's in there." He said, nodding to the holding tanks.

"Just make sure you find a cure for this thing okay, man? That's why they brought you, right? So you can fix it?"

"I'll do my best," Draven said. He couldn't think of anything more comforting or reassuring to say.

"What a way to go, huh? Survives the end of the world, killed by a shoelace. Just my luck."

"Hey, don't talk like that. As soon as we get Subject One into custody, we can start to work towards something resembling a cure." Kate said.

"Do me a favour," Herman said, looking from Kate to Draven. "If for whatever reason you don't make it... if something happens to stop you, don't let me turn. Don't make me become one of those things. I couldn't handle that."

"Come on, don't think like that," Kate said.

"No, I have to. Whilst I'm still me, I want you to promise me you'll end it if you have to. If it gets to that point where it's too late.... End it."

Draven nodded. There was nothing else to say.

"Okay, then I suppose you better put me in, just not with the angry one."

The three of them walked to the second of the holding cells.

"Alright, I'm ready," Herman whispered, keeping a close eye on the rotting, shambling thing inside. "Man, I hope it doesn't stink in there," he muttered, trying to force another smile.

"But what if we're wrong?" Kate said. "What if he's not infected and we put him in there with that thing?"

"That's a good point," Draven replied. "Maybe we should wait and see if you start to change."

"No," Herman said, pulling the release lever to open the door. "We all know I have it."

"Wait!" Kate said as Herman slipped inside the cell.

"Lock it, do it now," Herman said, keeping a close eye on the shambling creature as it shuffled towards him.

Kate didn't respond, she could only stare open mouthed. It was Draven who reactivated the locking mechanism. The door slid closed with a pneumatic hiss. Draven and Kate watched as the dead man shuffled towards Herman, who backed into the corner.

"I told you, it's going to attack him!" Kate said,

reaching for the release lever.

"Wait," Draven said, grabbing her wrist. "Give it a second."

The dead man pinned Herman into the corner. He cowered away, flinching as it leaned close and sniffed him. They were all still, all silent. They watched as the dead man retreated away from Herman, paying him no attention as it continued to shuffle around the perimeter of the cell. Draven and Herman locked eyes through the glass.

"That confirms it," Draven replied. "He's infected."

Herman read Draven's lips, then sat cross-legged in the centre of the cell and put his head in his hands. Kate and Draven returned to their seats. Neither acknowledged the silent sniffs as Kate cried. Draven only hoped the extraction of Subject One was on schedule and going to plan. With nothing else to do, he returned his gaze to the microscope.

CHAPTER TWENTY-THREE

Temporary United Nations refugee station

Shahapur, India

When word of the attacks on Mumbai first reached the leaders of the world, one of the first military operations was the securing of the city Shahapur, and protecting it from whatever force was invading. As the largest town in the Thane district and the source of most of the fresh water pumped to the city of Mumbai by its four immense dams, Shahapur was a key defensive position. The outer perimeter of the town was a living breathing barricade of soldiers and army personnel, as military vehicles from the various forces of the world combined to deflect the threat of Joshua's growing army. A truck rumbled towards the only entrance to the city which hadn’t been barricaded. The truck rolled past the fortified checkpoint, tracked all the way by the dusty, pale green T90 tank. It truck came to a halt, triggering the waiting soldiers into action. They opened the gate at the rear and ushered the people onto the ground. Suvari was close to the rear and was one of the last to be helped from the dark of the truck into the muggy, mid-morning heat. She paused and looked around, and realised all wasn’t as it seemed. Those who had been trapped with her weren’t being assaulted or murdered as her imagination had guessed but instead given water and food. A man walked towards her, carrying a bottle of water. He had kind eyes, tanned skin, and a beard growth which looked a couple of weeks old. His shirt bore the emblem of the United Nations, and it dawned on her that rather than captured, she had just been saved.

"Here, drink this," he said as he handed her the water. "It's hot, the last thing you want is to dehydrate."

She didn’t argue and took the bottle gulping at it.

"Easy," he said, grabbing her arm. "Just sip it. You'll make yourself sick."

"Who are you?" she said, taking gentle sips from the bottle like he said.

"My name is Anderson. How are you feeling?"

"How do you think?" she snapped. "Nobody told me anything when they brought me here. Your people are intimidating."

"They have to be. It's hard to separate the people from the others. We have to be efficient and make decisions quickly. No offence intended."

"Are you in charge here?"

"Uh, kind of."

"Kind of?" she repeated.

"Yeah, the commander assigned to rescue patrols was killed yesterday whilst defending a raid. I was next in the chain of command."

"But you're not in overall command? Who is in charge of this operation?" she said as she screwed the lid back on the bottle.

"I don't think that has anything to do with you, ma'am," Anderson said.

"My husband works for homeland security. I need to contact him."

Anderson averted his gaze.

"What is it?" Suvari asked.

"Homeland Security is gone. It was attacked a few days ago and burned to the ground. There's nothing left."

Suvari felt her legs buckle. Anderson grabbed her arm. "Are you okay? Go ahead and sit down."

She perched on the rear of the truck. "All this time, I was hoping to make contact with him. He warned me not to come, I didn't listen. Why didn't I listen to him?"

"Look," Anderson said, as he glanced over his shoulder at the rest of the makeshift camp. "The guy we have in charge right now came from there. He might know your husband. I'll take you to him."

"Thank you, I appreciate it," she said, still numb with the idea that Marcus might well be dead. She didn't think she could handle it, and so forced herself to be positive. "What is this place?" she asked, looking around bullet-pocked buildings which were filled with soldiers and civilians who were busy with various tasks.

"It's a safe place. That's all you need to know right now."

"I don't feel safe, no offence. I'd feel better out of the city."

Anderson frowned. "I take it you don't know how much shit we're in?"

"What do you mean?"

"Wait, let me backtrack here. What do you know

about what's happening?"

"Not much. I was in the city, giving food and water to some of the poor children when everything started to happen. Fire, screams, explosions."

"The city? Wait, you were in Mumbai?"

She nodded. "I rescued as many of the children as I could. A man tried to help us, but..." she lowered her head. "He didn't make it."

"Not many people did. You're the first we've had who survived the attack on Mumbai. You're a very lucky woman."

"I don't feel lucky," she whispered, seeing the grotesque faces of her rapists swim into her mind's eye. "What happened? Who has attacked the city? Why isn't the rest of the world coming to our aid?"

"I hate to tell you this, but as far as the order of importance goes, we're way down the list. Everything has gone to hell."

"It always does, the government here aren't known as the most efficient."

"No, not just here. Everywhere."

Suvari stared at him, not quite able to understand what he was saying but frightened all the same.

"Look, I hate to be the one to deliver the bad news.

Believe me, it already looks like you've been through hell. But I think you need to know what the situation is here. These attacks aren't just happening here, they're happening all over the world. The White House in America has been attacked and taken over; nuclear bombs have been dropped on Paris, Berlin, Tokyo and New York. All over the world, capital cities are falling to these people. We lost contact with the government here two days ago. We can only presume they are dead or captured."

"What about the army, surely there must be some resistance?"

"It's spread thin. We're losing people every day. Plus with the communication satellites down, coordinating anything is proving next to impossible."

"So what happens now?"

"For now, we stay where we are. We have food and water. We're hoping to start extracting people by air just as soon as we have word of where to take people."

"Are we safe here?" she asked.

"We're doing our best," Anderson replied, which was hardly an encouraging answer. "For now, we're doing okay. We repelled three raids in as many days. These invaders want in so they can control the water supply, which is the very reason we're doing everything we can to keep them out."

"Can I ask you a question," Suvari said, still avoiding eye contact.

"Of course."

"When the soldiers brought me here, they asked me if I was bitten."

"Don't worry about that," Anderson said.

"And then in Mumbai, I saw a man, a dead man who got up again when it should have been impossible."

Anderson looked away from her, watching a team of soldiers unload medical supplies from a truck and move them to a building. "It's true," he said, looking at her. "The dead are...coming back."

"You mean like..."

Zombies.

She couldn't bring herself to say it, even though she could think of no better description.

"Zombies. You can say it," he added with a wry smile which was a whisker away from a grimace. "Crazy I know, but that's what we're dealing with."

"How can it be?"

"It's this virus. Whatever it is, it's so powerful that it's not allowing the dead to stay that way."

"Can't it be stopped?"

"We have to hope it can be," Anderson sighed.

"You don't sound convinced."

“We’re in the dark here. Improvising day to day until we hear from someone higher up the chain. You know, we could use someone like you around here. The way you helped those kids and got out of the city alive shows you have some tenacity. We can use that."

"I’m no soldier," she said, unscrewing the water bottle and taking another sip.

"I didn’t mean to fight, we have plenty of people for that. What I need you for is to help with the civilians and the children. Not just the ones you rescued, but the others too, the ones who were already here."

"You mean you want me to distract them, to keep their minds away from how hopeless it is here?"

“Not at all. We could use someone who knows what they’re doing, that’s all.”

"I’ll do it, of course. That's why I came back to this country, to help people. I'll do whatever I can. I just want to know what here is. This is a lot to take in."

Anderson nodded. "Okay, let me show you around the camp and give you the tour. I can’t take too long, though, as we need to be prepped by nightfall."

"What happens then?"

"If the last few nights are anything to go by, that's when they will attack."

“The men from the city?”

Anderson nodded. “Yeah, they want the dam. We suspect they want to blow it. They’re burning crops and fields. It’s just another tactic to cause fear.”

“Surely you can’t fight them off. I’ve seen what they can do.”

“We can and we have. We have a good defensive position here which helps us. We’ll continue to do it for as long as we can.”

“Sorry, I didn’t mean any offence.”

“No, it’s okay, I’m in a shitty mood today. Tell you what, how about I take you to the commander, see if he can help you with any information about that husband of yours?”

“Thank you, I’d appreciate that.”

“It’s this way, come on,” Anderson said, leading her deeper into the camp. She paused to check that the children were okay, and was happy to see they were being given food and water; some were being wrapped in blankets. She followed Anderson towards the centre of the camp. Anderson led her into a green tent. She blinked, letting her eyes adjust to the gloom. It was set up as a makeshift office, the heat stifling despite the fans set up to move the stifling air around a little.

Commander Mathers was skinny, a narrow moustache on his top lip. Despite the fans rotating on his desk, his face was slick with sweat. Maps and documents were spread across the table, and he looked very much like a man under a lot of pressure who didn't have a lot of answers.

"What is it, Anderson?" Mathers said.

"Sorry, Commander, it's a bit of an unusual request."

"Spit it out. I'm up to my eyeballs here."

"We picked up a civilian, she says her husband works for Homeland. I just wondered if you might know of him."

Mathers looked past Anderson to where Suvari stood by the tent entrance. "A lot of people worked at Homeland. What is your husband's name?

"Atkinson, Marcus Atkinson."

Anderson and Mathers glanced at each other. "Director Atkinson?" Mathers said.

"Yes, he was in charge there."

Anderson grinned. "Today is your lucky day. I know

exactly who and where he is."

"He's here," Mathers cut in. "He came out to help with the aid effort."

Relief overcame Suvari, so much so that she couldn't breathe. "He's here? Where is he?"

"Anderson?" Mathers said, glancing at his colleague.

"He's just come back from a supply run. He's sleeping."

"Then I suggest you wake him. I imagine these two are keen to be reunited."

II

Sleep was a luxury he would no longer experience, a small price to pay for his survival. He had staggered back to the camp, covered in blood and delirious. He knew no others would return, and so he told those in charge what they needed to hear, that they had been ambushed and fought back as best they could, but everyone but him were killed. They tried to tell him he was brave, that he should be proud of himself for fighting, but the truth chewed through the lie with ease and filled him with an all-consuming guilt which he knew would never shake. He half hoped someone else would make it back and tell the truth of what had happened and put him out of his misery, but he knew that wouldn't happen. He had left those men to die when he could have tried to help. He lay awake in his bunk, staring at the roof of the tent and trying to remember who he was before, how his life was when he thought he was a man in control who could make the decisions nobody else could. He knew that man no longer existed and may never have existed at all. He was a sham, a character, someone who crumbled at the first test of actual bravery. He was scum and knew it.

"Marcus?"

He blinked, and looked towards the entrance to the tent, sure it was an illusion or some kind of waking dream. It was his wife. She stood at the entrance with Anderson. She was gaunt and bloody, but it was her.

"Are you real?" he mumbled under his breath.

She came to him. Already crying as she crossed the tent. It was only when they embraced, recalling the familiar feel of their respective spouse, did they truly believe that they were reunited. By some miracle, amid the chaos and the death, they had found each other. She was trying to talk, babbling incoherently. He couldn't listen. He was crying himself. They simply sat there and held each other. For a while, nothing else mattered, even the vile things he had done.

CHAPTER TWENTY-FOUR

Alan & Captives

Prison camp 124

Unknown location

The stench of death was thick and had ingrained itself into him. Alan had been at the camp for three days and was starting to think death might be a viable alternative to enduring any more of the hell he was experiencing. Exhausted, dehydrated and hungry, he along with four other fellow prisoners were transporting more bodies to 'the pit', a huge excavation which was half filled with the dead. Some had died through the punishing around-the-clock work schedules. Others had been older people with heart conditions or disabilities which rendered them useless to those in charge and were terminated. Some had tried to escape and had been brutally murdered, often in front of the watching masses as a means to prove a point and act as a deterrent. Just a day earlier, one man had been caught trying to scale the fences and had been led into the centre of the camp. There, in full view of everyone he was subjected to a horrific ordeal as Lucas cut off the man's feet and forced him to eat them, one toe at a time. Alan had watched, horrified and sickened as the old nursery rhyme raced around his head.

This little piggy went to market, this little piggy stayed at home...

The man sat there, blood pouring from his ravaged stumps, screaming and babbling as he crunched away at his own appendages. Lucas had watched for a while with some amusement, then grown bored and shot the man in the face. The man, however, didn't die straight away. He lay on his side in the dirt, twitching and somehow breathing through his one remaining nostril. One of Lucas's men moved to finish him off, when Lucas spoke up, making sure everyone could hear.

'No. Don't make it easy for him. This man should be left here as an example. He deserves to suffer for what he tried to do.'

Alan and the rest of the prisoners watched, waiting

for the man to die. When he didn't, and he just carried on twitching and snorting and bleeding, people drifted off and went back to work, many of them no longer wishing to watch the ordeal as it unfolded. Others watched for longer, Alan included, willing the man to give up and die. Eventually, they too went to back to work, leaving the twitching man to endure his slow, agony filled death alone. Alan hated himself for it, as he knew others of his group did too, but they returned to their duties as if the man didn't exist, walking past him without looking, trying to ignore the wet clucking noises coming from his throat. The man lasted all of the night and into the next morning before accepting his fate, and by then, Alan and the others were relieved, as to endure those death throes for any longer would have been enough to drive a man to madness.

Alan now had the man under the armpits, mangled face thrown back, one eye bulging out of its shattered skull as he carried him to his final resting place. Andy, the man who had helped Alan when he was captured, had a twin handful of his bloody jeans legs, the stumps within flopping against the material as the two walked to the smouldering pit filled with bodies. From the ridge above, Lucas's men watched.

"How's the mouth?" Andy said between breaths as they started downhill towards the pit.

"Itsh noth thoo badh," Alan said, still struggling to formulate words.

"It looks fucked up man, you must be hurting."

Alan nodded.

"Still," Andy added, glancing at the body they were carrying. "It could have been worse, you know?"

"I needh tho geth tho my wifth," Alan grunted, frustrated and angry.

"You know that's impossible. She's up there in the barn. I know it must hurt like hell man, but you need to let that go. It's over for her."

"I'd ftheel bether ifth I knew whath they were doingth in thhere."

Andy opened his mouth, then closed it and looked away. He almost lost his footing and grunted.

"Whath were you abouth tho sthay?"

"Nothin', just forget it."

"Ifth you know somethin' you shoudth thell me."

"Look, forget it all right? It won't help you."

"Ishn't thath my dethishion?"

They reached the edge of the pit, the rancid stench of burning flesh, hair and decay unbearable. They looked into it, the tangle of smouldering arms and legs making it impossible to tell how many bodies were there. Flies buzzed and darted like a cloud, an angry ever present drone.

"Fucking flies," Andy grunted as he let go of one leg wiping a grimy forearm against his head, leaving a dirty streak.

"Andhy..."

"Alright, alright, I'll tell you. Just don't say I didn't warn you. You won't like it."

"Thankth"

"Don't thank me yet. You haven't heard it. Before I say anything, let's do what we came here to do before these pricks put us down there with them."

Andy nodded.

"Alright, on three as usual. Ready?"

Another nod from Andy as they started to swing the corpse back and forth.

"One... Two... Three!"

They let go at the highest point of the swing, watching as the footless body tumbled down the side, arms and legs twisted like a ragdoll. He came to rest at the bottom in a half sitting pose, one leg tucked under him, the other stretched out in front, head lolling as if he were taking in the putrid aroma of his fellow dead.

"Jesus, I could have done without seeing that," Andy muttered. As they turned back and started to climb the hill, both were content to remain silent as they struggled with their efforts. At the top, the rest of the bodies waited. There were nine more in all. Keeping their heads down to avoid eye contact with their armed chaperones, Alan and Andy sucked in as much air as they could before grabbing the next body, disturbing more flies who were exploring the strange terrain of the dead man's face. This time, Andy took the heavier head end and Alan the feet. This one had been a suicide. He had hung himself with his bootlaces. Angry looking purple bruises around the skinny man's neck stood in stark contrast against his pale skin. On his inner bicep was a tattoo of the American flag erected in the debris of the World Trade centre attack, below which in swirling script was inked: 'Never give up'.

They remained silent until they were out of earshot of the guards, then, sensing Alan was about to ask again, Andy spoke.

"You remember the guy from the truck when we first met? Mike? The guy in the overalls?"

"The one who wath thalkin abouth thombieth?"

"Yeah, that’s him. Zombie guy. Anyways, yesterday, they sent him up to the barn."

"Whath fthor?"

"He's a mechanic, or, at least, he was in the old world. Anyways, they saw he had his uniform on and so they dragged him up there to look at a generator that was busted."

"He never saith anthigth,"

"Well, I asked him not to considering you're the only one of our group with a wife. Anyway, that’s getting ahead of the point. So they take him up there and show him inside to where this generator is that needs to be fixed, only Mike can't pay any attention to what these guys are showing him because of what they're doing in there."

"Whath isth ith?"

Andy swallowed as they neared the pit, the acrid taste of death thick in his throat.

"Anthy?"

"It's like some kind of breeding house," He blurted, flicking a quick glance to Alan and then looking away again.

"Whath do you mean?"

"He said they have all the women in there, right?

And they're strapped upright on these tables. Legs apart, arms above their heads. They're..." he hesitated, glancing again at Alan, who was watching him. "They're naked, all of them. Mike said they all look the same, heads shaved. What happens is, the men, they go in there and they take turns at having their way with them. Mike said the noise was unbearable. They're trying to impregnate them, make them carry their seed or some fucked up shit like that."

"Rape?" Alan said, the word for once perfectly formed.

"Yeah, multiple times a day by man after man after man. They have them hooked up to these drips which feed them, keep them nourished. It seems like that's their sole existence. Mike said there are around fifty of them in there, each strapped to their own table, each a unique 'station'. He said above each is the word ‘Eve’ and then a number. Eve one, Eve two, that kind of thing. He said..."

Andy looked away, swallowing the words.

"Jusht shay ith," Alan grunted as his heart raced and visions of his wife danced around his brain.

"He was only there for a few hours, but even in that time he saw man after man come in and just... well, you know."

"Wath my wifth there?" Alan said in a near whisper.

"I don't know man, I don't know what your wife looks like. You should talk to Mike. He was there. He's going back up there again tomorrow, so if you can describe her, he might be able to tell you. I'm sorry man, I really am. I hated to have to tell you this."

Alan barely heard him. He was thinking instead of how little use it would be for him to try and describe his wife in a way that Mike would understand, especially if all the women had shaved heads. He knew he would need to get there himself. He had already lost his children. Even if it cost him his own life, he was determined to get in there and set her free.

II

Later, after their exhausting eighteen hour work day was done, the men were allowed to rest. Ushered into large communal buildings which they had constructed, the men were, for the next five hours able to relax in the best way they could. With no beds to sleep on and given meagre scraps of food and just enough water to keep them ticking over, the cabin was filled with ghoulish, terrified faces of the weary who rested where they could, some sitting, others lying down. Some, like Mike and Andy, were still strong and seemed to be coping with the new regime. Others were struggling to handle both circumstances and workload. Alan thought it was interesting how easy it was to see who was strong and who was weak, and he thought he could gauge how long many of them would last. Ignoring his aching body, Alan sat on the floor next to Mike. He said nothing, simply staring straight ahead at the opposite wall.

"Andy said he told you about the barn," Mike said, glancing at Alan. "Whatever it is you have in mind, you should forget it."

"I need to geth in there. I neeth to sthee for mysefth."

"There's no way to get in there. I understand why you want to, but believe me, you don't need to see that."

Alan closed his eyes, dislodging the tears which he had so far held back. "She's all I hath letht."

Mike glanced at him, then turned away. "Believe me, the best thing you can do now is forget about her. I'm not telling you that to be an asshole, but for your own good."

"How can I forgeth? Sheth my futhing wifth,"

"Hey, take it easy," Mike whispered, ignoring the few glances which came their way. “I'm just trying to help you."

"Then geth me in there."

"And say I do, then what?" Mike snapped. "If by some miracle you get in there and see her, what then? You will still be in the same position as you are now, only you will have seen how fucking horrific it is and won’t ever be able to get the image of it out of your head, that’s the best case scenario. Worst case is they catch you and make an example of you. That Lucas is a sadistic son of a bitch. You know that as well as I do."

"Itsth worseth noth knowing."

"No, it isn’t," Mike replied, finally looking at Alan. His eyes were wide and white in the gloom. "I don’t think you get what it’s like in there, so as much as I don’t want to re-live it, I’ll do it to stop you from doing something stupid."

Alan waited, only half sure he wanted to hear what was to come.

"As bad as we think it is out here, with the death and the fear, it's nothing compared to what those women are going through. When I was in there fixing the generator, trying to ignore the screams and the begging,

I counted thirty six men who came in there and did things to those women which were borderline inhuman. One poor woman on the station nearest to the generator, Eve station twenty, was raped eleven times just whilst I was there. Eleven. The girl only looked to be in her early fuckin' twenties at best."

Mike had an audience now, curious ghouls who hung on every word. He went on, knowing if he stopped he would never tell it.

"As if the sight of it wasn't bad enough, the noise is worse. Those men come in and they pound away. It's violent, it's brutal, they swear and they kick and punch. Some of the women squirm and try to fight back, but the men seem to like that more. Another thing too. It's hot in there, really hot. The smell of sex and fear is overwhelming. It's like hell on earth. I'm not a man easily disturbed or upset, but the sight of those women is one of the most tragic things I've ever seen, even after everything that has happened. I'm not a violent man, not by any means, but I swear that if I had the chance, I would kill every last one of those women and put them out of their misery just so it would end their suffering. That's why, if you're asking me to help you, the answer is no, and nothing you can say or do will change my mind. I'm sorry, but I hope you understand."

Alan didn't respond. He did understand, and knew all too well whatever he was about to do, he would have to do alone. Without a word, he lay on the floor and turned onto his side. He had no intention of sleeping. Even if he had, he wasn't sure he would be able to now with Mike's words ringing in his mind. Instead, he started to formulate ideas and plans about how he could get up to the barn and see his wife.

CHAPTER TWENTY-FIVE

Draven & Kate

Underground Lab

The Pentagon

Washington DC, USA

They worked in silence, deciding it was better than discussing what had happened with Herman. They were surrounded by the reams of paperwork liberated by Herman as they looked for anything that might help them gain a head start on finding a way to stop the virus. The lights flickered on and off, and Kate gave them a nervous glance.

"That's the third time in half an hour."

"Relax, we're safe here. We're way below street level."

"Don't you wonder what's going on up there?" she asked.

He looked up from the paper he was studying and saw how afraid she was. As a man not accustomed to the finer intricacies of the female psyche, he grunted and turned his attention back to his papers.

"Well?" she pressed.

"I know as much as you do," he said with a sigh, giving her his full attention. "It's safe to say it's hell out there. We're in the safest place we could be."

"Sorry for speaking." she said and turned back to her console.

"I didn't mean to snap at you. The stress is starting to take its toll."

"It's fine. I get it," she replied, glancing over his shoulder to the holding cell where Herman still sat on the floor as his cellmate shuffled his endless circles. "We're all feeling it a little.I just wondered if there was anyone else out there apart from the ex-wife and kids who you were wondering about."

Draven shrugged. "I don't have any family, or at least, none that I speak to anymore."

She nodded, getting the impression these were skeletons which Draven didn't particularly want to uncover. To her surprise, he carried on speaking.

"My mother left my father when I was just a boy. I don't remember her, and my father kept no pictures. She's like a ghost to me. I do sometimes wonder if she's still out there in the world, although if you're talking about emotional connection, then no, I have none."

"What about your father?"

"He passed away when I was eleven."

"I'm sorry."

"We knew it was coming. He was diagnosed with Parkinson's disease. I was away from home a lot during that time studying at university, so I missed the symptoms. Worse was that he didn't want to bother me when I was busy with my studies. By the time I noticed there was something wrong, the illness was in a quite advanced state. He fought it, of course. In the end, he took a tumble down the stairs when I was in China on an expedition." Draven swallowed, his eyes staring through the wall as he recalled the long-buried memories. "There was nobody there to help him. He'd broken his leg in the fall and he couldn't get up, or drag himself to the phone to call for help. It was three weeks before the neighbours noticed the smell. By all accounts, he suffered a slow and painful death. Of course, nobody could find me to tell me, so it was another month before I found out. By the time I'd managed to get home, he was already buried. If there is one regret I have, it's not being able to remember the last thing I said to him followed by regret at not being able to say goodbye."

"That's awful, I'm so sorry," Kate said.

"After dad died, I dived headlong into my work. In the end, after it killed my marriage too, I decided it was better if I just stayed on my own."

"That must be a lonely lifestyle."

"I'm used to it. I think I'm just one of those people who is destined to be alone."

"You never know what could happen, though. You might meet someone else."

"I try not to think about it. It's-"

The lights flickered again, followed by a dull rumble of a distant explosion.

"Are we under attack?" Kate whispered, hand going to her weapon.

"No, I don't think so. It sounded distant. Away from the building."

"Another nuke?"

A vivid image came to Draven's mind then. He saw

Kate and himself heading upstairs to speak to the President, to find the building gone, blasted into oblivion by a nuclear explosion.

"No," he said, shaking his head. "We'd have felt a hell of a lot more if it was. Maybe it was a plane crash or something."

Kate nodded. "Strange how something which would be seen as a huge disaster a few days ago seems so trivial now."

"That's what happens when mankind gets thrown into the dark ages. Perspectives shift."

"What about-"

The lights flickered again and then went out. They sat in the dark, listening to the air conditioning unit power down. Draven was about to ask Kate if she thought there was a backup generator when the room became bathed in a dull red glow of the emergency lighting. It was then they both heard the dual click of the magnetic locks on the holding cells disengage. Draven's heart felt as if it had leaped into his throat. He was up and moving before he could think about it, charging across the room to the first cell. "Kate," he grunted, noting she was already following suit. He reached the cell just as its furious occupant slammed into the door. The steel frame hit Draven hard, winding him. He shoved with everything he had just as the muscular arm of the imprisoned soldier breached the gap, snatching, and clawing at Draven, who did everything he could to avoid the potentially lethal grasp.

Kate joined him, shoving against the door and jamming the prisoners arm. Infuriated, the captive screeched and grunted, pounding and slamming against the frame.

"Get some help in here!" Draven grunted through gritted teeth.

Kate lurched towards the lab door, shaking the handle. "I can’t get out, we must be on automatic lockdown."

Draven was about to reply when the door slammed against him. He almost toppled over, and somehow kept his balance and slammed his shoulder against the frame. "We need some help in here, now."

The prisoner now had his face wedged in the gap between door and frame, eyes wild, drool hanging from his chin as he snarled and snapped. He grabbed a handful of Draven’s shirt, tearing it from his shoulder.

"Don’t let him scratch you!" Kate screamed.

"We need more bodies in here!"

As he said it, the power came back on, bathing the room in its usual stark white lights. The power to Herman's cell came back online, the lock clicking into place. The split second distraction was all the prisoner needed. The door slammed open, knocking Draven to the ground. He looked up in time to see the snarling brute launching through the air towards him, teeth bared, eyes wild. He landed on Draven, knocking the wind out of him as he tried to bite at his throat. Kate grabbed him around the neck, but was shrugged off and sent sprawling across the tile floor. Draven's mind raced with the information he had digested, all of which made him incredibly aware of the danger he was in. A single scratch or bite, even blood or drool entering his mouth would lead to inevitable infection. He grappled with his opponent, arms trembling under the strain as his much bigger adversary clawed and scratched.

Kate sat on the floor, frozen and unsure how to react. It was the first time she had witnessed the frenzy of these creatures up close. Part of her had always seen them as human, but now she could see only beast. A violent force of nature which was single minded in its thirst for destruction.

"Kate."

She turned to the voice, locking eyes with Herman as he stood at the glass, yellow veins standing out against his pale skin. "Let me out, let me help him."

She shook her head.

"Come on, I'm still me. I'm still in control. I can help. I'm strong enough to fight him."

She looked at Draven, who was still wrestling on the floor by the holding cell. Every instinct told her not to release Herman. She was aware from the research they had done that the infected were almost a singular entity, and would work together to achieve their goals. She feared that by letting him loose, he would attack her and help his fellow prisoner to finish off Draven.

"No," she said, drawing her weapon and pointing it at Draven's attacker.

"Wait!" Herman screamed, banging on the glass. "You can't do that."

"Why?" she grunted, adjusting her aim.

"The blood. It could get in his mouth."

She lowered her weapon, feeling helpless.

"Kate, let me out. I swear to you I'll help him."

She stared at him through the glass. She saw no lie in his face, no evidence of deception. At the same time, she couldn’t ignore the prominence of the veins as they stood out on his cheeks and neck, the first signs of the transformation.

"Why should I trust you?"

"Because if I'd wanted to escape, I'd have done it when the power went down. Please, he doesn’t have much time."

Kate nodded, and before she could change her mind, unlocked the door. Herman stepped out and paused inches from her.

"Be ready to close the cell door," he said as he strode towards Draven. There was no hesitation, he grabbed Draven's attacker under the arms and lurched back, dragging him up and back into the holding cell. Kate sprinted to the door, slamming it closed and engaging the locking mechanism. She slumped to the floor, exhausted and shaken by the experience.

"Are you okay?" she said to Draven, who was still lying on the floor, breathing heavily.

He sat up, sitting against the opposite wall, eyes wide and filled with the same fear she could feel growing inside her.

"Whose blood is that," she asked.

"You already know the answer to that," he replied.

She crawled over to him, not sure her legs would be able to steady her. Draven's chest and shoulder were covered with blood. On his shoulder blade she could see the bite, twin crescents which bled freely.

"I tried my best to hold him off," Draven said, his voice cracking. "He was strong."

"I'm sorry," she said as she slumped back to a sitting position. "If I'd have acted quicker..."

"Let's not dwell on that right now. There's no point. I think we both know what needs to happen."

Draven got up, wincing at the pain in his shoulder. Blood, stark red against white tile dripped from his wounds as he walked to the glass to look at Herman. His perpetually angry cellmate was silent, perhaps sated by the taste of blood on his lips. Herman was pacing. He looked at Draven and grinned, and expression which melted when he saw the ugly wound on his shoulder.

"Oh man, please tell me that's not what I think it is."

Draven nodded.

"Doc, I..."

"It's fine. I wanted to thank you for helping me. It means a lot."

"If only things had worked out better for us both," Herman said. Then he approached the thick glass, his voice sounding flat and listless as it was relayed by the microphones built into the cell.

"Doc, I want you to do something for me. A final request."

"What do you need?"

"This virus. As much as I'm doing my best to fight it, I can feel it starting to take over. I don't want to be like him." Herman jabbed a thumb over his shoulder. "I always said I wanted to be in control of my own fate. I can't do that now, so I'm asking you to do it for me."

"No," Kate said, joining Draven at the glass.

"Come on, it's obvious by now it's dangerous to keep his kind... our kind alive. What happens next time the power goes out? What if my cellmate here gets out and decides to chew on the President?"

"That won't happen," Kate said, blinking back tears. "We can..."

"He's right," Draven said, trying to ignore the agony in his shoulder. "We can't risk this happening again."

"We can't just give up on him."

"Come on Kate, this is bigger than any of us. We have to respect his wishes."

"But we-"

"It's okay," Herman said, even managing a smile.

"This is what I want."

"Well I can’t watch," she said, striding away from the holding cell.

Draven and Herman stood, separated by a few inches of reinforced glass. "Who would have thought it would come to this, eh doc?"

"Yeah," Draven said, looking down at the floor. "I'm sorry I got you into all this."

"I was already involved. You don’t owe me any apologies, man."

"You just let me know when you're ready. You know, to...go."

"I’m ready now, Doc. I don’t want to experience this anymore. I don’t want to become one of these monsters."

"You realise what will happen to you don’t you? When I purge the cell."

"Yeah, I read the reports earlier. I know what's coming."

"It will be agonising."

"I don’t feel anything anymore doc. That part of me is already changed. Please, just do it before my mind goes too."

Draven nodded, struggling to hold back his own

emotion. He clenched his teeth and approached the control panel on the front of the cell. Above the speaker panel was a red handle inside a glass door. Printed in white above the panel was a single word.

PURGE

Draven opened the door and grasped the handle.

"Hey Doc," Herman said as he stood in the centre of the cell.

"Yeah?"

"Tell Kate I said thanks for trusting me. She'll know what it means." Herman folded his arms. "Okay doc, I'm ready."

"I'll see you soon, Herman," Draven said, then pulled the handle before he lost his nerve.

A siren started on top of the cell, a red domed light rotating in warning. Inside, a series of gas fuelled nozzles erupted to life filling the space with flames and ensuring every inch of the cell was purged. There were no screams. Draven was thankful that he could no longer see his friend amid the inferno, and could only stare into the fire as the heavy steel doors slid into place over the glass, locking in the fire which would reduce both inhabitants of the cell to nothing. Draven turned to Kate, looking at her across the room. No words were shared. He could see her cheeks streaked with tears.

"You know the drill," he said as he walked to the second cell. "Lock it as soon as I'm inside. I'll stay with you as long as I can be helpful. With luck, I'll still be able to assist when Subject A arrives. Until then, better to be safe."

He unlocked the cell door, striding into the space which Herman had earlier shared with the shambling dead thing. Numb and unable to comprehend what was happening, Kate followed him and activated the locking mechanism watching the door slide into place. She watched through the glass, hoping against hope that Draven might not be infected. Like Herman before him, Draven waited for his rotting cellmate to approach and assess him. The dead thing leaned close. Draven made no effort to fight. The dead thing sniffed, its face inches from Draven's, then it backed away and continued to circle the cell. It was all Kate could take. She strode away, tears blurring her vision as she pounded on the lab door and screamed for someone to let her out.

CHAPTER TWENTY-SIX

Alan & Captives

Prison Camp 124

Location unknown

Alan had withdrawn further into himself. He went about his tasks, which used to horrify him so much, with a distant indifference to them. It was like they were being performed by someone else. The dead no longer concerned him, nor did his own well-being or mortality. All that mattered was the barn. He had kept a close eye on it during the course of his daily duties, just as Mike and Alan had watched him. He knew they were distancing themselves from him, and he didn't blame them. It would be better for them not to be associated with him any longer. He had accepted the idea of his own coming death with much more calm than he might have expected. He supposed with so much already lost, he didn't much care what happened as long as he did what he needed to do. Even another gruelling eighteen hour day of transporting the dead to the pit couldn't dampen his excitement or determination. He operated on autopilot, almost able to forget where he was and what he was doing, to forget how much pain he was in, both physically and mentally. He could almost even forget that whilst he worked, his wife was probably enduring unimaginable horrors at the hands of their vile captors. With the day now done, he ensured he was one of the first to get back to the cabin so he could get prime position closest to the door. Without a word, he lay on his side facing the wall and closed his eyes. As exhausted as his body was, he wouldn't allow sleep to take him. Instead, he listened to the sound of his weary fellow captives shuffle into the cabin ready to be roll called and then taken to get their meagre supply of bread and water. His plan was flimsy and there was a good chance it wouldn't even work, however with no other options, he was desperate enough to try. Finally, after what seemed like an age, roll call came. As always, two of Lucas's men came to count heads before they were taken to gather their rations. There were always a few who didn’t go, and they were the ones who invariably didn’t last much longer.

"Hey man," Andy said, shaking his shoulder. "Come on, you need to get something to eat."

Alan didn’t answer, nor did he look at the closest thing to a friend he had. It pained him to do it, but he feared if he did, Andy would see what he intended to do.

"Hey, come on, try to eat something."

"Leave him." One of the guards snapped. "His loss if he doesn’t eat."

Andy did as he was told, and joined the others as they were led out of the cabin. Alan waited until they were gone, and sat up, looking around the room. Other than him, there were around six other people who had declined to go for food, and he was grateful none of them were paying any attention to him. As casually as he dared, he stood and slipped out of the door before he lost his nerve.

II

The orange glow of dusk lit the work yard, which was heavy with shadows. Up the hill, the farmhouse where Lucas and his men spent their nights was ablaze with light which spilled from the windows. The dull thump of music rolled towards where he stood in the shadow of the cabin, his eyes now focused on the barn. His plan was as insane as it was simple. His intention was to walk straight to the barn and hope nobody stopped him. If they did, he planned to tell them he had been sent there on an errand. He was aware such action was dangerous, and could result in a swift and painful end to his life without him ever finding out if his wife was safe. Something came to him then as he stood there, a crippling and absolute fear. He knew he was relatively safe in the shadows, and to step out into the relative light of dusk would mean there was no turning back. He tried to remember his children and yet he was so exhausted, so drained that he couldn't recall their faces. He didn't even think he would be able to move, and would be found when the others returned from getting their meagre rations, cowering in the darkness and unable to explain why he was outside. It was the thought of what was happening to his wife which spurred him into action. He hurried across the yard, hands in the pockets of his dirty jeans, trying to look both casual and invisible at the same time. Ahead, the barn loomed large, a golden letter 'I' spilling out of the gap where the doors met. He kept away from the farmhouse, conscious of the fact he could hear Lucas and his men laughing and talking as they feasted and drank. The consequences of them finding him didn't bear thinking about. It was all or nothing. Live or die. He skirted around the periphery of the light spilling from the farmhouse, keeping close to the shadows and unable to believe his luck that nobody had been outside to catch him. He knew all it would take would be a guard stepping outside to smoke a cigarette and he would be done for. He supposed he ought to thank the arrogance of Lucas and his men. So certain were they of their rule based on fear, they didn't accept the notion one of them might dare disobey orders.

He reached the barn, the hulking structure towering above him. He half expected to see a cruel twist of fate to deny him, perhaps a lock on the door or some kind of an alarm. It seemed, however, his luck was holding out. There was no lock, and he could see no wires which would lead him to think there was any kind of alarm system either. Before he could lose his nerve he inched open the door and slipped inside.

CHAPTER TWENTY SEVEN

Underground Sewer base

Iraq

Akhtar watched his brother as he played with some of the other refugee children, and couldn't shake the feeling of terror which lived inside him. The idea of going into battle scared him, as did the thought or remaining behind and being powerless to do anything until the others were either victorious or failed. Either way, he knew things for his brother would change forever. Since losing touch with their parents, Akhtar had felt a huge sense of responsibility towards his sibling, as if it were his job and his alone to protect him, even though he himself was just a child. Too many sleepless nights had been spent wondering what the future would hold for them both and the wider world in general. He was so preoccupied with his thoughts that he didn't notice Branning sit beside him. Like the rest of them, he was jaded and had lost weight. He tucked his knees up under his chin and watched Akhtar as he, in turn, watched his brother.

"You know it will be time soon," Branning said in basic Arabic. "We will be moving on the camp."

Akhtar said nothing.

"I know you must be afraid. We all are. It's just…." Branning let his words fade. He was no good at this kind of thing. He had no children nor did he have any idea how to speak to one, let alone to tell him how he was expected to risk his life in a probable suicide mission.

"Can we win?"

Branning was caught off guard by the question. He squirmed, feeling Akhtar's eyes on him.

Lie or tell the truth?

He wasn't sure but knew the longer he delayed the more likely the boy would suspect the answer was no.

"We intend to try our best. That's all we can do."

"Why don't we run? Why do we stay here?" Akhtar said, his lip trembling. He looked away from Branning and stared at his brother, blinking through the tears which welled in his eyes.

"Look around you. There are innocent people here. Lots of them. People like your brother. We can't go into the streets and move them. It's too dangerous. But if we can take the camp, we will have shelter. Supplies. More importantly a communication network. We have to try."

"Surely we can just stay here. They haven't found us yet. Maybe they never will." Youness said, palming away the tears.

"They haven't found us yet, that's true. But what happens if they do? We have nowhere to run. No way of escaping. This was only ever a temporary solution. We have to make our stand."

"I'm not a fighter. I don't know how to shoot a gun!" Akhtar hissed.

"Look, I understand-"

"Just leave me alone. Please." The boy turned away, showing his back to Branning. The soldier sat for a moment, unsure if he should say anymore. He noticed Hamada standing by. He wasn't sure how long he had been there, but was watching both carefully. Branning nodded and Hamada waved him over. Branning complied, crossing the room and leaving Akhtar alone.

“Is there a problem?” Hamada asked.

“It’s the kid. He’s afraid.”

“With good reason. His survival chances are slim.”

“Jesus, do you have to be like that?” Branning said.

“It’s the truth. Surely that is better, is it not? Would you rather lie to the boy?” Hamada said, keeping his dark gaze on Branning.

“I wanted to give him hope.”

“Fear of death is a much stronger motivator, Branning.”

“I’m sorry, I disagree.”

“That is up to you. All I know is how my own kind responds. It is very different to your American ways.”

“Then you talk to him.”

“Very well.”

Hamada walked past, Boots clunking on the ground. Curious, Branning watched as Hamada sat in front of Akhtar, blocking his view of Youness. Hamada watched the boy, eyes dark and sharp.

“Are you afraid?” Hamada asked.

Akhtar nodded.

“For you or for your brother?”

“What do you mean?” Akhtar asked.

“Do you fear death for him or for you?”

"For us both. I… I need to protect him."

Hamada nodded and folded his massive hands over his knees. "And what better way to protect him than fighting for his freedom?"

"I'm no soldier. I'm just a boy." Akhtar shook his head and glanced around Hamada to his brother.

"You have been shown how to use weapons whilst Branning and I were away, correct?"

"Yes."

"I'm told you were quite good."

"But I'm not a soldier. I don't know how to fight."

"What is your name?" Hamada asked.

"Akhtar."

"Let me tell you a story, Akhtar. A story about a boy not much older than you. He lived in a village in the hills. A simple place. Quiet. Peaceful. The children of the village longed for adventure. For excitement. The elders of the village frowned at this. They understood how fragile peace was, and how every day with it was one to be blessed."

Hamada paused, noticing that some of the other children had stopped playing and were now listening to his story.

"One summer day, the boy and his friends were sent

to fetch water from a well. It wasn't far, just a few kilometres outside the village. The children did as they were asked, each taking a pail to fill from the well. The day was hot, and the way difficult. Rocky terrain, little protection from the sun. The children, however, were used to such conditions. The five of them went without complaint, making for the well."

Even Branning was now watching with intent as more of the children surrounded Hamada, sitting in a rough circle.

"They reached the well a little after the middle of the day. Each boy drank his fill, relieved to taste those cooling waters. They filled their pails, each to the brim with water. This, they realised would be the most difficult part of the journey. They way back would have to be negotiated during the hottest part of the day and with the extra weight of the water to burden them. Still the boys did not complain. They walked in silence, heads bowed against the heat, concentrating on the way ahead. They didn't notice the bandits coming up behind them. They were of the same age, but unlike the boys from the village, these were more akin to a pack of wild animals. They stole from the weak, robbing those who were too afraid to fight in order to survive another day of biting and scratching out and existence."

Hamada smiled, and Branning noticed there was no humour in the expression.

"The bandits cornered the boys at the mouth of a valley. There were only three of them, but they were bigger and carried knives to go with their dangerous attitudes. The bandits demanded the boy's water. As they had been taught, the boys from the village tried to reason with the bandits. They offered them a full pail of their own if they would grant them safe passage. The bandits, however, were not so easily swayed. Each of them wanted to impress their friends, and laughed at the offer. One of them pushed one of the boys from the village to the ground, his pail breaking open and feeding the precious water into the thirsty ground. The fate of the second boy was the same. He too was knocked to the ground, his water spilled."

Hamada leaned closer, telling the story only to Akhtar despite his new audience.

"Two of the other boys say what was happening, and handed over their pails, backing away to avoid the same treatment of their friends. The bandits now had enough water, yet they still craved more. One boy from the village remained, standing defiant, placing his body between the bandits and the pail in order to protect it. The bandits demanded he hand it over. The boy or course was frightened. His heart raced like a hundred galloping horses, and his body trembled with terror. Yet, he didn't move, nor did he break the gaze of the bandit he had deemed to be the leader of the group. The bandits demanded the water again, telling the boy he would be sorry if he didn't hand it over. The boy was immovable. He had worked too hard, toiled too long to get the water to just give it away to these bullies. The three of them surrounded him, intimidating the boy. Yet despite the absolute fear inside him, he didn't remove his eyes from that of the leader."

"What happened?" Akhtar asked.

"The bandits attacked the boy. Beat him. He fought back, of course, clawing and scratching, refusing to let the bandits beat him down. Bloodied and beaten, the boy refused to stay down. More to the point, he refused to give the boys his water. Eventually, perhaps seeing that the boy was not as easy to dissuade as his friends, the bandits fled. Taking the two stolen pails with them, but leaving the boy and his alone. Bloody and angry, the boy still found it in himself to smile."

"Why? He was beaten. They lost almost all of the

water." One of the children said.

Hamada turned to answer but was cut off by Akhtar.

"No. the boy stood up to them. Although they lost some of the water, he still won."

Hamada nodded. "Yes, that is correct. Although four of the five pails they had been sent for were lost, the one saved by the boy who refused to back down in the face of fear was, to the boy, at least, the sweetest, most flavoursome water he had ever tasted."

"What happened to him? The boy I mean." Akhtar asked.

Hamada held his arms out to his side.

"It was you?" The boy asked as the other children looked on.

"This is a story from my childhood. The boy from the story grew into the man sitting before you. You see, Akhtar, fear is a good thing. It reminds us that we are alive. I see in you the same bravery which I was forced to show to those bandits."

"I don't want to die," Akhtar whispered.

"I understand. We are all afraid. But we must fight. We will fight against these monsters who force us to live underground like animals. We stand together, Akhtar. Boys and men, soldiers and civilians. We fight as one. We stop only with victory."

Hamada stood, looking at his audience. "I won't tell any of you not to be afraid. I know that beast already gnaws at you. All I will tell you is that together, we will stare it in the face and defeat it. All of us together. All of us united. For now, rest well. Soon it will be time to be counted."

Hamada walked away, eyeing Branning as he crossed the doorway where he stood. Branning grabbed his arm as he passed.

"Hey."

"What is it, Branning," Hamada sighed."

"Thanks. For doing that, I mean. I think you got through to them."

Hamada looked as awkward receiving praise as Branning was in giving it. The two men locked eyes. "Come," Hamada said. "We have much to discuss."

Branning followed Hamada towards the makeshift war room, trying not to think about how many of the children who had just listened to Hamada's story would survive the pending assault.

CHAPTER TWENTY-EIGHT

ALAN

EVE BARN

PRISON CAMP 124

The first thing that hit him was the smell, closely followed by the intense humid heat. Like a one-two punch from a skilled boxer, the twin blows left him reeling. The smell was a thick, pungent odour of sweat and sex with something else underneath, a coppery smell. Alan thought it was the smell of fear. He drew large gasping breaths against the unbearable humidity. It was only as he looked around the room that he saw why the temperature was so high.

It was exactly as Mike had said. The women were arranged in a semicircle and strapped upright to benches which were angled back. Their legs were spread and bound with thick leather straps, their arms likewise, pulled upwards and out. A memory came back to him then, a moment of beauty amid the horrors which now lived in the darkness of his mind. It was of him and his son on Cocoa Beach in Florida, both on their backs in the sand and making sand angels, waving legs and arms with abandon, his son's giggles filling the air with their melody, a song joined by the laughter of his Anna, his beautiful Anna.

He blinked, those good times fading back into the soup of horror.

The naked women made no effort to ask for help. He looked at them, flesh slick with sweat, skin bloodied and bruised, the way in which they had been displayed both degrading and horrifying. He let his eyes drift over them, hoping and dreading identifying his wife in equal measure. He had almost started to hope she had been spared when he saw her. He inhaled a sharp breath, held it and slowly released it.

Anna.

His wife, the women he had fallen for quite by accident when he was an awkward college student. Anna who he had met by chance on a cross-town bus ride, the woman who he always felt was out of his league yet somehow they bonded. His soul mate, his rock. His Anna with the beautiful smile and slightly uneven shape to her eyes.

It was only those, the blue brilliance of them which he could recognise.

His Anna, the one he knew, was gone. The shell of a woman on Eve station 17 was something else. He was sure it was just someone who looked similar and tried to convince himself it was some kind of freak occurrence, and she had somehow managed to escape their ordeal. However, the illusion was easily broken. He recognised the tattoo on her shoulder, the birthmark on her stomach which they always joked looked like a pink, abstract map of England. It was her. Her blonde hair was gone, shaved off as with the other unfortunate souls she was with. From her up-stretched arms, wires snaked and were attached to drips administering fluids. In front of each woman was a small electric heater, each strung to the next in a snake of plugs.

"Bastards," he muttered when the pieces fell into place and he saw what they were doing. It was a form of torture. He could see it now, Lucas standing in the centre of the room, back straight, chest out, a sick smile etched on his ratty face. Basking in the control.

Revelling in the power. He could even hear his voice reverberating around the humid, sticky room, perhaps even repeating the same speech he had delivered to Alan and the rest of the men as they were bundled from their trucks.

'My name is Lucas, and I am in charge of this facility. Make no mistake. This is the safest place for you to be. Out there you face starvation, death, and the constant threat of attack. In here you will be given shelter and food in exchange for your hard work. Any attempt to escape will result in death. Any breach of the rules will result in your death. Any attempt to go against the authority of my men will result in death. Forget any notion that someone is coming to help you. They're not. Also, forget any notion that you can escape. You can't. The only way you will walk out of this facility is if I choose to let you. You are all now prisoners of a war in which there can only be one winner.'

Alan looked at the network of tubes snaking out of his wife's skin, although he was still, for the time being too afraid to approach. In his head, the phantom Lucas went on.

'You will be vessels, carrying the seed for my men.

Do not resist them. You are hooked up to IV lines which will provide you with your nutrients and hydration. If you do not, you will bake and wither in the heat. Be good to my men, they will allow you to receive that which you need. Fight or resist, your IV lines will be shut down. Believe me that is something you don't want to happen. The temperature in here is forty-eight degrees. Without fluids, you will be lucky to last three days. Do as we tell you, and you shall all survive.'

Alan felt a rush of rage at the cruelty, and although he had no idea if the scenes in his head actually ever played out, he wouldn't have been in the least bit surprised. He realised as he stood there in the sweltering heat, his shirt clinging to his skin that he was putting off the inevitable. He crossed the room on legs which he felt could give out on him at any time. Now within touching distance of his wife, it was all too real. It was all too easy to believe what had happened.

"Anna," he whispered, or maybe he just thought it. He was in a fuzzy, faraway place where he almost felt detached. His wife didn't respond, she hung there, head down, chin resting on her chest, skin like waxy silicon slick with sweat. He reached out to touch her, then recoiled, unable to go through with it.

"Anna?" he said, this time sure the words had left his lips.

She stirred, a flick of the head, yet she didn't look up at him.

"Baby itsth me," he whispered as the tears came, stinging his eyes and blurring the grotesque imagery in front of him. He lifted her head, her skin slick and hot. Her eyes lolled and rolled as if detached from their sockets. An ugly bruise covered her right cheek and she had a split lip, both injuries which were too fresh to have been inflicted by the crash before they were captured. He held her face, forcing her to make eye contact with him, and yet even when he did, her gaze was glassy and without recognition, which hurt him more than he could have ever imagined. It was then he understood the purpose of the IV lines. He traced them back, reading the bags hung by the side of each Eve station. Along with the nutrients and saline for hydration, was morphine. His eyes traced the line back to his wife's arm, where the needle was taped in place. It at least explained her lack of recognition. He could only imagine how easy it would be after such an ordeal for the brain to blow a fuse or two and maybe even shut down for good. This was a situation he could fix. If he could detach her from the morphine and get her outside, he half hoped they might be able to escape. He reached out to the needle in her arm when he heard Lucas's voice, although this time it wasn't in his head, it was outside the door.

"Whoever is in there, please come out now."

Alan felt fear, hot and explosive in his gut, which tightened into a tiny, quivering ball.

"Come out now, and I promise, you won't be harmed."

Alan couldn't see him, but even so, he could almost hear the sneer in Lucas's voice.

"You cannot escape. Exit now, and you will be unharmed. This is your final warning."

Alan hesitated. There was something in his brain, a revelation or idea he couldn't quite grasp. It was the feeling when an elusive name is on the tip of the tongue and won't quite present itself.

"Whoever you are, you are not in any trouble. Just come out now. There are men all around the barn. You cannot escape."

It came to him then, exploding into clarity.

Why don't they just come in and take me?

There were plenty of them, and he was no match for

them. He would have expected them to storm in and remove him with the same ruthlessness they had displayed from the start, and yet they were hanging back. Alan looked around the room at the women and understood. They were important, more than he might have ever imagined. He looked at his wife, absently wiping tears from his cheeks with the back of his arm, then took her face in his hands, leaning close, his forehead against hers. He could feel the intense, fever like heat from her skin.

"I wanth you tho undershtanth," he whispered, looking into her vacant lolling eyes. "Thith way ith the betht,"

He wanted her to respond. A nod, even just a moment of clarity to let him know she understood he was there with her and what he was about to do was a last resort.

"Look afthter the kidth, I'll be with you sthoon," he said, blinking away more tears as he kissed her on the forehead.

With a shaking hand, he reached out and opened the valve on her morphine feed, allowing it to flow without restriction. As he did it, his inner voice screamed at him that he was a murderer and what he was doing was wrong without even trying to fight. Another part of him, the one which was actually in control, argued there was no other choice, and this was the only way to end her suffering. As he watched and waited for his wife to die, another idea came to him. One which may even give him a chance at a little vengeance before he joined her in whatever came after. One thing he was certain of. No form of hell if it existed could be any worse than the horror he had endured so far. Wiping his eyes and giving his wife another kiss on the head, he looked around the room to see if there was any feasible way to put his plan into action. His eyes fell on the humming generator that Mike had been sent to fix. Despite everything, a very faint smile appeared on Alan's lips. The hammer sitting on top of it would do the job fine. He only wondered how many he would be able to free before Lucas sent his men in for him. His wife first, though. Just to be sure. He picked up the hammer, then, sobbing he swung it at her head with all the strength he could muster.

IV

Outside, Lucas stood, arms folded, legs spread as he

glared at the barn door. At his side, his second in command, a man as broad as he was tall by the name of Gabriel joined him. Behind them, more men waited, weapons drawn, ready for action as soon as the command was given.

"Let me go in," Gabriel grunted, red veins glowing just beneath his skin. "I'll get this worm out of there."

"No," Lucas said, his eyes fixed on the door. "We can't risk it. Joshua was very specific."

"There must be dozens of facilities like this by now, hundreds. We can afford the risk."

Lucas turned to Gabriel then, eyes full of venom. "And do you want to be the one to have to explain to Joshua that of all those dozens or hundreds of such camps, ours was the only one to be compromised? Have you any idea what he would do to us?"

"I'm sorry, I didn't think."

"No, and that, Gabriel, is why I'm in charge of this facility and not you."

"So what do we do?"

"We coax him out. Then I'll make him eat his own innards as I have every man under my command violate whoever he went in there to save in every way imaginable."

"That's not how the Eve programme works, it..."

Gabriel stopped speaking and lowered his eyes from the intense glare of his superior. Satisfied that he had regained control, he turned his attention back to the barn.

"There is nothing in there which can help you. Whoever you are looking for, a wife. A girlfriend. A lover. Whoever it is doesn't matter. They belong to me now. You should be proud. They are the future and will bear the first natural born generations of our race. When you and your kind are dust, Eve will live forever, immortal and worshipped the world over."

Lucas hesitated, wondering if he would have to risk sending one of his men in when the doors to the barn burst open.

VI

Alan took a deep breath, only half hearing Lucas as he delivered his sermon. Exhausted from his efforts, he shoved the doors open, no longer afraid of anything Lucas or his men could do to him. He stood in the door covered in blood with the light at his back, his shadow distorted and ghastly as it was thrown in front of him towards Lucas and his men, whose look of absolute revulsion made his efforts worthwhile. He knew his actions wouldn’t change things, not really. If anything, it would only be a minor hindrance. A brief setback. To him, however, it was a huge victory. Whatever happened next, the look on Lucas's face was worth all the agony he knew was coming to him.

Alan stood in the light of the barn door, chest heaving as he breathed in ragged gasps. The hammer hung at his side, bloody clumps of flesh clinging to its head and dripping to the dusty ground. Blood splatter covered his face and chest, the whites of his eyes standing out as he stared straight ahead, a twisted half-smile on his lips.

"What have you done?" Lucas hissed.

"Freeth them," Alan said, dropping the hammer to the ground. "Freeth them all."

Lucas's men hurried into the barn, closely followed by Lucas himself, who came to a halt in front of Alan, glaring at him. Alan looked right back, no longer afraid.

"I’ll make an example of you for this. You understand that, don't you?" Lucas whispered as he looked beyond Alan to the carnage in the barn. "You will suffer like no man has ever suffered before," Lucas said with a sick smile.

Alan smiled back, in turn causing Lucas to show a flicker of shock. Alan dropped to his knees and put his hands on top of his head. He waited until Lucas's men dragged him to his feet and into the farmhouse towards whatever fate awaited him. Alan closed his eyes, and couldn’t wait to join his wife and children in death.

CHAPTER TWENTY-NINE

Joshua & Genaro

Oval Office

The White House

Washington DC, USA

The White House had been restored almost back to its pre-takeover state. Apart from the bullet holes which riddled the walls and the glass which was missing from the windows of the Oval Office, it could almost still house the President. Joshua was staring out of the window at the world he now thought of as his own when Genaro knocked on the door and walked in.

"Joshua, we have another problem."

Joshua didn't turn from the window, nor did he answer. He remained in place, arms clasped behind his back. Genaro waited, unsure if he should speak or not.

"Go on," Joshua said, still staring out at the White House lawn.

"We have identified something else which could bring everything you've built crashing down."

"Oh?" Joshua said, turning to face the withered scientist. "And, much like the Richard Draven situation, I ask myself why am I only learning of this now?"

"I'm sorry, it was an oversight. Something I didn't expect to be an issue."

Genaro stared at the carpet, doing everything he could to avoid the intense stare of his superior.

"Spit it out, doctor," Joshua said with a sigh as he sat at his desk.

"Remember when we first started the Apex project and you were the first to be administered the virus?"

"Don't call it that," Joshua snapped. "Virus is such a negative word. This is our gift."

"Our gift, then," Genaro said, clearing his throat. "When we first started our trials, you were so receptive to the serum, so compatible, that it rendered our previous subject as obsolete."

"Previous subject?" Joshua said, showing a real interest for the first time. "Doctor Genaro, you told me I was the first."

"The first success, yes, that much is true. Before you, however, there was another."

"Who?" Joshua snapped.

"Just a man. It was an early version of the vi... Serum. He lasted only a few sessions before we moved on from open trials to closed."

"And why did you stop?" Joshua said, his voice low, the sinister edge unmistakeable.

"He wasn't compatible. Not like you. Whereas your system took and adapted to the programme, his... resisted."

"Resisted?" Joshua repeated.

"Yes. He rejected the change."

"What you're telling me, Doctor Genaro, is that you thought it was unimportant to tell me there was someone out there who was not only resistant to our gift but might be able to be used against us?"

"I'm sorry, I didn't expect this to happen so quickly. If I had I-"

"Where is he?"

"We had him moved. Transferred to a secure prison in England. I didn't think he would ever be found."

"But?"

"We intercepted intelligence which says there is an operation ongoing to extract him. I came straight here to tell you. We have some men a few miles from the location we can-"

"Destroy it."

"Joshua, we don't need to do that. I can get some men to take care of this."

"No. I don't want to take any chances. I want a nuclear device dropped on that prison right away. I don't want to risk anything being left to be used against us."

"Joshua, please. I have family who lives within the blast radius it-"

"Family? And what are we?" Joshua said, standing and leaning on his desk. "Did I not make you part of my family? My inner circle? Is my generosity not enough to you?"

"No, of course not, it's just that my son, my grandchildren are-"

"Their deaths will be swift, my friend. Take solace in that. Remember how we must sacrifice the ties of the old world in order to usher in the new."

Genaro pursed his lips, then looked out of the window, straining to hold back tears which were unexpected and unwelcome.

"Don’t mourn them, my friend," Joshua said with a smile. "Honour their memory. Know that for them, the suffering of the world is behind them."

"Of course, it’s just... This all feels so inhuman, Joshua. This wasn’t the intention of the project. When I started I wanted to save lives, not take them."

"You see us as monsters?" Joshua said, walking to the window.

"No, not monsters, it just all seems so...brutal."

"It has to be this way. This world is so corrupt, so broken, only a complete purge will suffice."

"Millions will die."

"Millions already have," Joshua said. "That doesn’t mean we can stop."

"Please, I have done everything you have asked of me, don't make me kill my own grandchildren."

"Had you told me of this sooner, I could have dealt with it differently. Now, you leave me with no choice. Let your guilt and anguish be a lesson. Learn from it, Doctor Genaro, or do not. Whatever you choose to do is your decision to make. My orders still stand. Destroy the prison, and do it now."

Genaro hesitated, then lowered his head. "Yes, of

course. I’ll give the command right away."

CHAPTER THIRTY

Parker, Stanhope, Trig & Ross

Belmarsh Prison Roof

England

"Fucks sake," Parker said, tossing the radio to the floor. "I still can't get through to anyone."

"We can't just stay up here," Stanhope replied as he checked on Trig, who was slumped forward, his bandaged neck soaked through with blood.

"Our extraction point was the roof. I don't know what else we can do."

Parker stood and surveyed the landscape. Slate skies made the silence of the surrounding streets even more ominous. There was no sign of activity of any kind. "I don't like this Stanny. It's too fuckin' quiet."

"I hear that. It's like a ghost town," Parker replied.

"I bet they've imposed martial law. People will be under curfew."

"Doesn't help us much does it. We need to get out of

here. Trig has lost a lot of blood, he needs a doctor. If our evac isn't coming, it looks like we need to do it ourselves."

"What about that?" Stanhope said, nodding towards the courtyard below.

Parker joined him and looked over the side at the abandoned police van in the car park, the driver's door open.

"Better than sitting here on our arses. Come on then, let's do it," Parker said as he stood.

"Where will we go?"

"Woolwich I reckon. Somewhere neutral where we can get our target delivered."

"What's so important about him anyway?" Stanhope said.

"Fuck knows, mate. Let's just deliver him and be done with it."

"Alright, sounds good. Let's move out."

They moved to the rappel lines, Stanhope and Ross helping Trig, who was struggling to stay conscious.

"I'll go first and see if there are keys in the truck," Stanhope said, unhooking Trig's arm from around his neck and leaving Ross to bear his weight. Stanhope clipped onto the rappel line and was about to climb down when they heard it. An ear piercing shriek cutting through the silence.

"What's that?" Ross said.

Parker and Stanhope exchanged glances.

"Air raid siren?" Stanhope said.

"Yeah," Parker replied. Both of them were thinking about the bombs which had fallen on Tokyo, Paris, Berlin and New York.

"Let's get the fuck out of here, right now," Parker said, grabbing Trig and moving towards the rappel lines.

"What is it? What the hell's happening?" Ross shouted, eyes wide as he stared at them and then out at the eerie silence of the city. "Where the hell is everyone?"

"Not now pal," Stanhope said. "Let's just get moving."

Parker helped Trig over the edge of the wall, clipping him onto Stanhope's line. He took the other rope, helping Ross over into position. All the while, the siren continued to blare and slice through the air.

Stanhope and Trig landed first as Parker talked Ross through using the rappel lines. They stumbled towards the van, Trig weak and barely able to walk, Stanhope going as quickly as he could, unable to shake the idea that they were about to be nuked into oblivion. He looked to the skies, knowing the heavy cloud cover meant any bomb that did fall wouldn't be seen until it was far too late. Stanhope opened the back of the van. Inside was a caged section with benches on each side of the van used to transport prisoners and keep them secure after arrest.

"Get in Trig, lie on the floor and for fucks sake keep some pressure on that wound."

Stanhope went to the driver's side, grateful to find the keys still in the ignition. He climbed in and started the van, the growl of the engine as it spluttered to life giving him renewed hope. Parker and Ross were now on the ground and jogging to the van. Ross climbed into the passenger seat.

"I'll stay in the back and keep an eye on Trig. You get us out of here," Parker said.

"Got it. Now hurry up and get in the back."

Parker did as he was told, climbing in and slamming the door shut behind him. Stanhope looked over his shoulder through the mesh cage into the rear. "Hold on tight, this might get bumpy."

Parker nodded, already applying more pressure to

Trig's wound. Stanhope put the van into gear and turned it around, flooring the accelerator as he raced away from the prison. With the streets deserted, his progress was unhindered as he made his way through the twisting streets.

They heard it coming, a deep rumble like faraway thunder coming at them. Although it was already flat to the floor, Stanhope pressed the accelerator even harder, the heavy van struggling to pick up speed. The sound built to an immense crescendo, then the flash of light came, illuminating the sky with intense brilliance.

Distracted and afraid, Stanhope misjudged his speed, the van slewing towards a shop window. He slammed on the brakes, tires screaming in protest as he desperately tried to slow their momentum. The van vaulted up over the curb and slid into the front of the florists, glass shattering as the van ploughed into it. Stanhope put the van into reverse, gears grinding as he tried to get the van back out onto the street. The rumble was loud now, an intense sound which was now reminiscent of an earthquake. Stanhope looked in the driver side mirror and saw the fireball racing towards them, its summit rising way out of sight. He drew breath as fear grasped him just seconds before the van and its occupants were obliterated to a molecular level by the blast which had destroyed the prison and everything else within a three-mile radius of it.

CHAPTER THIRTY-ONE

Pentagon War Room

Washington DC, USA

Kate watched from the operations room with the President, Bill Watson, and his team as the screens which had been giving live video feed from the cameras on Parker and his team's body armour cut out, filling the screen with static. The room watched in silence, unable to comprehend what had happened. Watson left the room, leaving the President and the others in a shocked state of disbelief. Watson re-entered the room, his face pale and listless. He sat down heavily in his chair beside the president.

"Detonation on London confirmed sir. No survivors."

President Carter nodded and rubbed his temples, then turned to Kate.

"Go and speak to Mr. Draven, see if he can suggest anything that might help us."

"He's infected sir, besides, he said this was our only chance."

"I know that. Ask him anyway," Carter snapped. "Right now anything will help."

"Mr. President," Watson interjected, "With all due respect, we need to forget Richard Draven. It's only a matter of time until the change takes place. We need to look at our other options."

"We don't have any other options, Bill. In case you haven't noticed, we're getting our asses kicked."

"All due respect sir, but we can't give up."

"Exactly, which is why I want to know if Draven can help us any before he changes."

"I don't think I can do it," Kate said. "I can't look at him knowing he hasn't got long left."

"I hate to be blunt Miss Goodall, but it wasn't a request," Carter said. "Draven knows you. He trusts you. If anyone can get him to help us, it's you."

"It might already be too late. This thing can be fast acting, sir."

"Then don't waste any more time talking to us."

Kate stood, feeling the eyes of everyone in the room on her. "Yes, Sir."

She left the meeting room, heading for the elevator to the lab, unsure if she could bring herself to look Draven in the eye, let alone ask him for help.

II

The silence of the elevator was bliss, and part of her wished she could just stay there, listening to the comforting hum of the light set in the roof. However, it was not to be, and the doors slid open. She walked to the lab, half hoping he was already changed so she wouldn't have to question him, and then hating herself for thinking it. Pushing the door open, she went inside, giving a cursory glance to the still sealed holding chamber in which Herman's life had ended. She opened the intercom channel in Draven's cell so they could communicate.

"It failed, didn't it?" Draven said, seeing the haunted look in her eyes.

She nodded.

"Subject One is dead?"

Another nod.

"If you can get a tissue sample, some form of DNA from the body, maybe we can use it."

"No, that's not possible."

"Why?" Draven asked, already suspecting the answer.

"They must have known, they must have realised what we were doing."

"They intercepted the extraction team?" Draven said, wincing as he shifted position.

"You okay?" she asked.

"Yeah, shoulder hurts like hell. Forget about that, though. What happened to Subject One?"

"They dropped a nuke. Obliterated London. There's nothing left," she said, hating how cold she must sound. "Now the President wants you to suggest what we do next."

Draven went cold. The words didn't sink in for a few seconds, and when they did, he had no idea how to process the information. "Then maybe he should be down here to ask me himself."

"You should be careful what you wish for," President Carter said as he walked into the lab, Watson at his side. "Mr. Draven, I'm sorry for what's happened to you. I realise that asking Miss Goodall here to do the job I should be doing is equally wrong. As you heard, our extraction mission has failed. Now I need you to give me some kind of alternative plan before you change into one of these...things."

"Kate said a nuke went off in London. I need to know you got my family out safe."

"Your family were extracted, Mr. Draven and are on a plane heading here. Now please, we don't have much time. You have to give us something."

Draven paced in his cell, trying to process the information he had taken in, and finding the same outcome with every possible scenario. "I'm afraid I can't help," Draven said.

"There must be something you can suggest, anything at all," Carter said.

"You don't understand, Mr. President. This was our last shot, our one chance at fixing this."

"But there must be something you can do," Carter said, standing inches from the glass.

"There isn't anything I can help you with now, sir. Without Subject One, we can't formulate a cure."

"Are you saying there's no way to prevent this from spreading?" Carter said.

"I’m afraid so."

"Mr. Draven, we don’t have the resources to fight this, lives have been lost, more are extinguished by the hour. What am I supposed to do?"

"Frankly sir, I'd forget trying to fight this. Right now, I'd make survival the priority."

"We can’t just roll over and let these people win."

"They've already won, sir. I’m sorry."

The President was about to respond when Bill entered the lab. He hurried to the president, casting an uncertain eye on Draven.

“What is it, Bill?” The President said.

“Sir, it’s him. He’s made contact.”

“Joshua?”

Bill nodded and glanced again at Draven.

“Alright, I’ll come up to the war room and see what it is he wants.”

“Sir, he doesn’t want to speak to you.”

“What do you mean?”

Bill nodded at Draven. “He wants to speak to him.”

All eyes fell on Draven, who looked just as surprised as the rest of them. The President pondered for a moment and then turned to Bill. “Can he be patched through to the monitors in here?”

“Yes sir, but it will be video feed from his side only. He won’t be able to see you.”

“Good, I don’t want him knowing where we are or the situation we are in. Patch him through.”

Bill hurried away, leaving Draven and the President together. “Do you have any idea why he would want to talk to you?” Carter said.

Draven shrugged. “I don’t even know why he has any knowledge of my existence. I’m as confused as you are.”

“It’s on,” Kate said as the large monitor in the lab was filled with a close shot of Joshua’s face. He was calm and smiling, appearing untroubled by the destruction he had caused.

Carter turned to Draven, either unable or unwilling to hide his fear. “Best if you don’t mention your current physical state. Just to be on the safe side.”

Draven glanced at his bloody shoulder and nodded.

“Alright, patch him through.” The president said.

Everyone stood and watched, curious to see what Joshua had to say. His grin widened and he addressed the room.

“Richard Draven, at last, we meet,” Joshua said. Draven stood by the reinforced glass, watching the screen. "I wish I could see you and hear your reaction to what I'm about to say, but with the current state of the world, I'm afraid I will have to address you and hope you heed my words. Now, I imagine you are wondering what I could possibly want from you, a mere civilian. The truth is, that we both know the information you carry in that inferior brain of yours. Knowledge, as you know is power. I imagine you sitting there now amid President Carter and his staff." Joshua smiled and nodded. "Good. I think it would benefit them to hear this too. As you have by now witnessed, direct action against me and my family is ineffective and results in nothing but death and pain for those who try to perpetrate it. Your soldiers are dying on the streets. Your arsenal of weaponry is under my control. In any fight, it would be clear to see that my victory is assured. Even so, I know the nature of your kind. You fight on with the belief that you can still win, that you are still top of the food chain. You, Richard Draven, are apparently key to this."

Joshua hesitated, staring into the camera. "What should I do about this situation, I wonder. My plan was to eliminate you, but it seems in this, at least, your government got to you first and now have you hidden away somewhere. My next course of action was regrettable but necessary."

The camera shot zoomed out, giving a wider view of the presidential office. Joshua stood behind three chairs. On them, Draven's Ex-wife and two children were sat. Draven felt his legs quiver, and an icy fear tighten his gut into a ball.

"You said you had them. You said you had saved them." Draven said, glaring at the President, who for once had no answer. His lips moved, but no words came out. Now everyone was staring at him, looking for an explanation. On the screen, Joshua went on.

"I can only imagine what you are feeling right now, Richard. Fear. Shock. Possibly even betrayal. I'm sure your great leader told you your family was safe, that they were in good hands on their way to take part in a grand reunion with you." Joshua shook his head and put a hand on Leanne's shoulder. She flinched, her eyes streaked with makeup. In the back of Draven's mind, he noticed that his ex-wife had changed her hairstyle. Joshua went on. "This, Mr. Draven, is why I want change. This is why I had to take action, to rid the world of politically motivated liars who would tell you anything you wanted to hear in order to get results. Me?

I'm not like that. With me, you get absolute honesty. For example, I'm sure you are curious about the fate of your family. Your ex-wife, Leanne, Your son Ethan and daughter Imogen. A lesser man, a man like President Carter would tell you they would be safe and unharmed, just like he told you he was sending his men out to retrieve them. Trust me when I tell you, that there was no attempt to do this. When my men picked them up and brought them here there was no protection, no help. Your president lied to you, Richard. Just like he lies to his country."

Draven glared at Carter again, the fear now morphing into a rage. The President was pale and gawping at the screen open mouthed, struggling to take it in.

"I'd like to tell you they weren't afraid, Richard. But I'm not a liar. I won't do that. I want you to know that they are all scared and confused, and worse of all they don't know why other than it's because of something their father did. That's sad, isn't it?" Joshua ruffled Ethan's hair, the young boy flinching away. To see it hit Draven hard. They were all terrified.

"I would ask you to cease all assistance to them, Richard, if I thought it would suffice to get the desired result, but I know the government, and I also know President Carter. He would either coax you or imprison you and force you to help anyway, which could yet happen. What I want to do is to remove the will for you to help. I want you to know, Richard, that the blood spilled today will not be on my hands. It will be on the hands of the man who told you your family would be safe."

Draven knew what was coming, but refused to believe it. When it happened, the speed and brutality was numbing to him. Joshua pulled Leanne's head back by the hair, at the same time bringing the knife in his other hand up and dragging it across her throat. Blood, more than Draven ever imagined possible to be in a human body sprayed out, cascading down her clothes and spattering the children, who in turn screamed.

In the lab, Kate looked away, Carter was still staring in dumb shock at the images on the screen. Draven could see his ex-wife twitching as Joshua pushed her head forward, more blood spilling out of her. He saw Joshua's lips moving but didn't hear what he was saying, his own screams blocking out the audio. Carter, however, could hear it all. he could hear the incessant drip of blood, the last remaining gurgles as life ebbed from Leanne, the terrified screams and sobs of the children who had been forced to witness their mothers murder and, of course, he could hear Joshua, who was still calm, still untroubled.

"I'm sorry you had to witness that, Richard. Truly I am. I'm sure your president will try to console you and tell you that no man deserves to see his family die, yet thinks nothing of sending wave after wave of soldiers out to wage wars in order to benefit him and line his pockets. As I said earlier, none of this is my fault, nor yours. This blood is spilled by your president."

Draven fell to his knees and pounded the glass as his son's cries were silenced by the blade. The shocking imagery too much even for the president to watch. He turned away, feeling numb and sick, surer than ever that he was out of his depth, and had no business trying to run the country. Draven stared at the screen, blinking through a glassy film of tears as Joshua shoved his dead son, the sound of his fragile body hitting the floor incredibly clear and loud.

"Please….Please, stop…." Draven moaned. He thought he was going to throw up. Nothing mattered anymore, nothing in the world meant anything to him. He watched as Joshua put a hand on Imogen's shoulder, blood-spattered knife glistening in his right hand.

“And then there was one. You might not believe this, but I truly am sorry it had to come to this. I hate death as much as anyone. But sometimes, a point needs to be made that leaves little doubt.”

“Draven pounded his fists on the glass. “Don’t, please, don’t do it. She’s just a kid she’s just a….”

The words were lost on the way from brain to mouth as Joshua cut Imogen’s throat and shoved her off her chair. Draven could only stare, his mind filled with static, like he was barely tuned into himself from some distant place. He watched as Joshua stood behind the body of his ex-wife. The blood no longer pumped out of the body. Draven knew she was dead. In that moment, he realised he still felt something for her. It wasn’t love, that was long gone. But a huge sense of sadness that she would no longer be in the world. Joshua put the knife on his desk, then placed his hands on her shoulders. Somehow, he managed a smile. “I trust my point has been made. Stay out of this, Richard Draven. Soon enough you will be reunited with those you lost.”

The screen dimmed and went dark, and silence enveloped the lab.

"Let me out."

Both President Carter and Kate looked at the broken figure on his knees in the cell.

"Richard…." Kate said, then stopped speaking. There were no words that could help.

"Open the cell Kate. Let me out." He repeated, still staring at the floor.

"I can't do that. You have to understand."

He lurched to his feet and slammed his fist on the reinforced glass. "Open the fucking door and let me out!" she flinched at the ferocity of his scream, and her hand moved towards the door controls.

"Don't do that, Miss Goodall. Think about why he's in there."

"You," Draven said, turning to stare at the President. "You told me they were safe. You said they were on their way here. You lied to me."

"Mr. Draven, try to understand…."

"You let them die!" he screamed, wiping the tears from his eyes.

"It wasn't like that."

"Wasn't it? You tell me what I want to hear so I'll keep working. That's how it sounds to me."

"Mr. Draven, I know you're upset, but try to

understand…."

"Upset? Let me out of this cage and I'll show you how upset I am. You let my family die."

"You forget your place, Mr. Draven. I'm the leader of this country. Although I would have gladly sent someone out to retrieve your family we just didn't have the resources. Granted, we had no idea things would escalate in such a way, but I'm the leader of this country and have to act in its best interests."

"He was right." Draven shook his head and wiped snot and tears across his face. "This is just a political agenda."

"That's what he wants you to believe. This man is guilty of genocide on a global scale."

"Fuck you."

"Mr. Draven, you can't speak to me like that. I run this country. You need to show me the proper respect."

"I have no respect for you. Not anymore. Because of you, my family is dead."

"Mr. Draven, tell us how we can stop him. Tell us what to do."

Draven turned away and sat on the floor in the centre of his cell, facing away from the President and Kate, unable to bear looking at them any longer. For a moment there was silence, nobody sure what to do.

"What now, Sir?" Watson said to the President.

"Nothing.It's over."

"Over? We can't just give up the fight sir." Bill said.

"We need to turn our priority towards survival," Carter mumbled.

"I'm unclear on the directive here, Sir."

"There isn't one, Bill. The game is over. He's won. All we can do now is try to live through this and hope for some kind of miracle."

"And what about the people? There are millions out there who are counting on you to find a way to fix this."

"They're on their own. We can't help them any more than we can help ourselves."

"I can't accept this sir, I can't believe you would just give up like this."

"I'm sorry, Bill. I know this is hard to accept, but this is how it is. Get to your family and do whatever you can to survive what's to come."

Watson looked at the president, then at Draven in the cell. "You can't just give up, Sir."

"I'm sorry, Bill. There's nothing more I can do." President Carter walked away, leaving Bill and Kate alone in the lab. They looked at each other, then at

Draven, then they followed the president out of the lab, both of them trying to ignore Draven's cries as they were amplified around the room.

III

Above ground, power grids all over the city went down leaving cities cloaked in darkness. In the White House, Joshua stood at his window, looking out over the orange glow of fires as they raged across the skyline. Genaro stood by the wall, camcorder hanging at his side, face pale as he stared at the bodies of Draven's family on the floor, their blood staining the blue carpet almost black.

"Was that necessary, Joshua? They were children."

Joshua didn't turn from his view. He had decided he liked the city so dark. Without the harsh artificial light, it looked beautiful. "It was necessary. There can be no room for weakness."

"But they were so young."

Joshua turned towards the older man. "You disapprove?"

Genaro lowered his head. "It's not my place to question your decisions."

"But of anyone, I value your opinion. After all, you are, in essence, my father. Without you, I could not be what you see before you."

"Whatever you feel is right, Joshua."

"Look at me."

Genaro didn't want to, but free will was something he no longer had. He lifted his head and met his master's gaze.

"What I did may seem shocking and unnecessary, but in order to break the resistance of those who oppose us, it was necessary. Do you think of me as a monster?"

"No, of course not," Genaro said, the bitter taste of fear lingering in the back of his throat.

"Do you see me as a foul beast who would steal life from those so young?"

Genaro lowered his head, hoping he wouldn't be pushed to answer.

Joshua crossed the room and gently touched the doctor's leathered face, causing him to look up. Their eyes locked. Genaro couldn't help but notice that Joshua was still spattered with blood.

"I've disappointed you, haven't I?"

Genaro was too afraid to answer. Joshua let his arm

drop to his side.

"Yes, it seems I've disappointed you a great deal."

"My grandchildren are a similar age," Genaro said. "Children shouldn't suffer for the sins of their parents."

Joshua smiled. "Your wisdom is of great benefit to you, my friend. Perhaps you are right."

Joshua walked to where the children lay on the floor. He crouched by Ethan and turned the boy over onto his back, his pale skin and dead-stare confirming that there was no life in him.

"So beautiful, even in death, aren't they?"

Genaro couldn't bring himself to look, but knew he would have to answer. "Yes, they are."

"So innocent. So ready to be moulded into something else." He turned to face Genaro. "Do you believe in chance, my friend?"

Genaro shook his head, relieved to be asked a question he could answer. "No. I never have."

"I agree. There is no such thing as chance. Take this boy, for example. See how I have cut across his jugular? Death would have been quick and assured."

Joshua then went to Imogen, and again crouched before rolling her onto her back. Even though her neck was savaged, she was still alive, her breathing shallow and eyes filled with fear as she stared up at him. "See the difference, my friend?"

Genaro was compelled to look and felt his stomach somersault at such an awful sight. He nodded

"See I only cut the soft flesh. The main arteries were avoided. You could say it was by chance or fate, or you could suggest it was deliberate, that perhaps it was my intention to prolong the child's death, which itself leads to a new question. What kind of god of the new world would I be if I didn't have power over life and death?"

He gently touched the child's blonde hair, brushing it away from her eyes. "I *am* a god, and I can choose who lives and who dies."

"Joshua, please, put the girl out of her misery. She doesn't deserve this." Genaro said, his face twisted into a mask of disgust.

Joshua took the bloody knife from the table, then returned to the girl. "It would be so easy to extinguish this flame, and yet I find it difficult to do so. Perhaps this is a clear sign that I should have a child of my own, someone who I can teach in the ways of the new world."

Genaro looked on, unable to hide his horror as Joshua cut his own wrist. He watched the blood drip down his forearm to his elbow, then onto the child's lips and into her mouth.

"As a God, I have decided the child shall live, and will be raised as my own as we go into the new world. Draven's daughter dies today, and mine is born."

Genaro left the office as Imogen's neck wound started to heal. He didn't see it, but as he left he could hear her as she greedily drank the blood offered by her new father.

EPILOGUE

The lab was in darkness. Although the tears had gone, the gulf of emptiness within him had grown. He still sat cross-legged on the floor, head in his hands. He listened to his body, waiting for the first signs of the change he knew was coming. Nothing mattered to him anymore. The chaos the world as in was irrelevant. With the loss of his family, only hate and vengeance filled his mind. It was as he was thinking of this that the locking mechanism for his cell released. He looked up at the door, then over his shoulder at the glass. Beyond it was dark. He stood up and approached the window, looking through his own gaunt reflection. He cupped his hands to the glass and surveyed the lab. There was nobody there, but someone had been. The lamp at the desk where he and Kate had been working was switched on, and a box left on the table.

He walked to the heavy steel door and pushed it open, then stepped out into the lab. He held his breath and listened, wondering if it was a trick, then realising he would never get a better chance, hurried to the box on the table. Inside were four things. At the bottom was a security guard's uniform. On top of that, were two paper folds of money. The third object was a black handgun and four clips of ammunition. The final item was a handwritten note. Draven took it out of the box and read the uneven scrawl.

Put this on and wait for the alarm.
You deserve your revenge.

He looked again around the lab, then got changed, stripping off his old clothes and getting into the guards uniform. He made a bandage of sorts for his shoulder to stop the blood seeping through then stuffed the gun and money into his jacket. The uniform was a little small, but it would suffice. He walked to the lab door, wondering what would happen next when the fire alarm sounded. The shrill sound and red beacons echoing around the building. Seconds later, people started to file out of the building. Draven opened the door and peeked out. Amid the officials in suits, were guards dressed the same as he was. He took one last look over his shoulder at the darkened screen, which in his mind's eye was still filled with the images of the terrible things Joshua had done. Whoever had left him the note was right. He *did* deserve his revenge and thought he had an idea how to get it. He stepped into the corridor and joined the train of people as thy evacuated the building. By the time anyone realised what had happened, Draven was long gone and had disappeared into the night, his mind filled with ideas on how to make Joshua pay for what he had done. It was no longer a question of helping the human race. Now it was a question of vengeance.

TO BE CONCLUDED

www.ingramcontent.com/pod-product-compliance
Lightning Source LLC
La Vergne TN
LVHW021231080526
838199LV00088B/4308